MW01135091

Share the Road

by

Sean Day

To my parents, for everything.

I

When he finally came around, he realized he had crossed into California. No one knew where he was, and even he was sketchy about how he got here.

As he slowly came back from his latest fugue state, and his eyes refocused on the present, his other senses came back in a tingling wave like he had slept on them wrong. The air, heavy with early morning moisture, was infused with the scents of grass, pine and a hint of saltwater. Though thick with scents he could almost taste, the air was almost absent of sound. The only noises he could detect were made by him moving through the landscape. The morning was peaceful and potent, and he supposed he could forgive his mind for losing its grip.

He did a slow systems check as things continued to come back online. He pivoted his head back and forth and rolled his shoulders to release the knot of tension. As the perception of dull pain was once again noted by his awakening brain, he raised his butt out of the seat.

As he stood out of the seat, he dropped his heels to stretch out his calves and hamstrings. He leaned farther forward and dropped his chest toward the handlebars to increase the stretch. He fanned out his fingers and wiggled them without releasing his grip on the brake hoods.

The "Welcome to California" sign, canary yellow lettering on a peaceful blue background, is what brought him back around. The cursive writing was much less formal than the block lettering on the "Leaving Oregon" sign across the street. He briefly considered stopping to take a picture of it, but that felt a little too touristy. He still wasn't sure how many souvenirs he wanted to return with.

Though he had been riding for only a short time this morning, he had already been on the road for more than a week. He was well beyond any distance he had previously ridden on his bicycle, and he still had some 500 miles to go if he was to end up where he was initially aiming. The destination held no specific meaning to him, but he needed something out on the horizon if he was going to continue to move forward.

Even though he felt no desire to photograph his crossing of state lines, he pulled over to the side of the road anyway. He wanted to take a break to stretch his legs, arch his back, and let his mind continue the waking up process. Though riding a bicycle is one of the most relaxing things he does, physical tension knots up in a place just above his shoulder blades if he is not careful to pause once in a while. Lately, his mind seemed to be susceptible to cramping as well.

The morning was a few hours old, but there was still a bit of mist lingering from the fog that settled in overnight. Still leaving his camera in his bike bag, he wandered along the roadside, his gait slightly awkward from his hard-soled biking shoes. The repeated hours and days on the bike, coupled with the chamois pad in his shorts had him walking bowlegged like a trail-worn cowboy.

Much of his route so far had been along highway 101, hugging the coastline of the Pacific, but today's ride had brought him inland for a bit. Shades of blue and white were replaced by lush greens, and the surrounding trees seemed to cling to the morning's mist for dear life. Soon enough he would be baking under the sun, but for now, the cool morning reminded him of home.

As he walked along the shoulder, kicking a particular stone like all men seem to do, thoughts began to push through the veil. They came unbidden in flashes of pain and regret, and he did his best to push them away like so many noisy children. Occasionally, he would open the floodgates and let emotion wash over him, but he did his best to postpone these moments until he was prepared to be caught in the undertow. He prided himself on his ability to control his emotions, but lately it had begun to falter.

He had been on the road for about a week now, and things had not improved. He felt different somehow, in a subtle way he could not describe to anyone else, but he wouldn't call it better. His inability to explain things, even to himself, was one of the reasons he left his world behind for a while.

He could not face his friends and family right now. He knew that many people would think he was running away from what had happened, and he could only half-heartedly disagree. He didn't imagine that the answers would suddenly appear out here on the road, but he knew it was even less likely if he had stayed to face judgment.

The melancholy ramblings of his mind were not helping or abating while he walked, so he figured it was time to get moving again. As he turned back, leaving the kicked rock a few hundred yards down the road, he suddenly remembered an old Peanuts cartoon by Charles Schultz.

His mind felt like a network of severed lines and synapses. No matter how hard he tried to remember how everything spun out of control, he couldn't call it up. Yet this twenty year old memory of a forty year old comic strip comes to mind with no effort.

As he remembered it, Charlie Brown is walking along the beach with Linus. Charlie Brown picks up a stone and throws it into the ocean. Linus comments that the stone endured years of tumbling and tossing through the thrashing surf to finally make it to shore, only to have someone casually toss it back in. Charlie Brown being who he is, now feels guilty. About a rock. Our rider, Michael, has almost an equivalent capacity for guilt, but at least he doesn't extend it to the rock he was kicking. Not exactly a sign of progress, but the thought made him briefly smile.

As he walked back down the road, he looked at the bicycle that had carried him all this way. It was nothing special as far as road bikes go. People can spend $10,000 or more on a bike if they have that amount of disposable income, and the belief that an expensive bike will make them better riders.

His bike was a step above the entry model, and he found the best combination of components he could get for the $1,200 he spent. He had to take on a side project in order to afford it, so in a relative sense it was as expensive as a $10,000 bike might be to someone else.

He had left the bike propped up against a speed limit sign. Bikes these days rarely come with kickstands, and quite often without pedals. It was an odd thing to discover when shopping for his ride, but now it made a certain sense.

There is a subculture obsessed with customization, and you can spend hours and thousands of dollars picking out components. Pedals and shoes work together as a system on road bikes, and there are several options to choose from, and even more opinions on which combination is best. Manufacturers don't even bother putting on a universal pedal, knowing it will only be replaced.

But beneath the minor tweaks an individual makes lies a simple machine largely unchanged over the last half century. There is an elegant beauty in the clean and spare lines of a bicycle. Delicately tapered metal is fused together to form thin triangles, the angular shapes contrasting with the two perfect circles of the wheels. Kickstands not only add weight in a sport obsessed with shaving off grams, but they clutter the clean lines of a work of art. It is like attaching a window crank to the frame of a painting.

Hooked to the back of the Michael's bike was a trailer with zippered mesh and fabric sides, built upon a sturdy metal frame and 20 inch tires. It was an anchor to the light, airy freedom of the bike. The trailer was well worn with use and covered with road grime. Though he originally bought it to carry his child, it now held a tent, sleeping bag, clothes, a backpack, and for no good reason, a guitar.

II

Returning to the bike and trailer, he did a quick check looking for anything obviously loose or out of place. Satisfied that nothing was amiss, he hopped back on the bike and rode out in search of some coffee.

A number of years ago, one of Mike's friends had ridden his Harley out to the annual Sturgis rally in South Dakota. His friend had mentioned that he always liked to get in an hour or two on the road before stopping for breakfast. This seemed to break up the day, and make it easier to get in the miles.

Mike had adopted this habit, using the promise of coffee as motivation to get in those first few miles. This actually suited his body more than his typical at-home routine. He found he enjoyed working up an appetite before eating the first meal of the day. It is only the need to eat before the commute to work that forced him to eat breakfast before he was hungry.

His breakfast of choice most mornings would be found in a greasy-spoon diner, but what he ended up with depended on what the next town provided. Sometimes he was lucky and his day would begin with bacon and eggs, but more often he had to settle for an espresso stand and whatever muffin or scone they had to offer.

Breakfast was also one of the few places for conversation out on the road. Lunch was usually in a burger joint or sandwich shop, and if he went anywhere nicer for dinner, waiters usually left him alone. But for some reason, breakfast is a much more chatty meal. Whether he stood outside a coffee stand, or sat at the counter of a local diner, the person serving coffee was much more warm and welcoming than anywhere else. Maybe it is the promise of a new day or just the caffeine hitting the bloodstream, but whatever it is, it seemed to hold true so far.

Mike was not a morning person, but he had begun to appreciate the increased hospitality of the coffee clan. Though the reason for the journey was to be alone for a while, he enjoyed the brief company of strangers that knew nothing of his story. It definitely helped that he had been awake and on the road for an hour or two before contact with society. Night owls and morning people do not mix well first thing in the morning.

This morning's route did not pass through a major city, but he found an espresso stand next to a gas station. Espresso stands often had clever names like "The Daily Grind", "Cool Beans" or "Brewed Awakenings". This one chose to use the popular mispronunciation and was named "Coffee Express Expresso".

The barista was an older guy that seemed angry to be there, so there would be no pleasant chit-chat this morning. In the few begrudging sentences he spoke, the man mentioned he was the owner and his regular employee didn't show up. Mike did not press for more, and he leaned against the back of the shack to enjoy his coffee and carbs.

He had been fortunate and hadn't been caught out in the rain during these outdoor breakfast stops. His gear was packed in waterproof bags, but his body was not as well protected. It is one thing to ride in the rain, which he had ample experience with, but another thing entirely to stand outside a coffee shack trying to eat a pastry before it becomes a rain-soaked ball of mush. There is a certain amount of satisfaction in weathering the elements to get where you need to go. Standing motionless in the rain implied you just weren't smart enough to go inside.

After a decent Americano and a bland scone, Mike took advantage of the gas station restroom to clean up a bit. After a week on the road, he had begun to tune into the free services as they passed by.

After taking care of business, Mike turned to the sink to clean up. He was a little surprised to see an actual mirror above the sink. More often it was one of those sheets of polished metal that can't be shattered by vandals, and only gives you a distorted glimpse of yourself.

There was no style to his closely cropped hair, so he rarely spent time looking closely at his reflection. When shaving, his focus was on the movement of the razor, and there was no real evaluation of how he looked when he finished.

But this morning he rested his hands on the counter and leaned toward the mirror to take a hard look at himself. His face was still pretty youthful, though it had been at least a year since anyone paid him the subtle compliment of carding him for a liquor purchase. His dark brown hair had gone gray at the temples, the whiter shade spreading more rapidly over the last year. He was reasonably fit for a man just turning 40, but his cheeks had a certain fullness that kept him from being considered thin. The love handles didn't help much either.

As he considered his reflection, his eyes went out of focus. He looked through the glass like he was trying to find a hidden image in those stereogram pictures popular a decade before. He wondered where all the time had gone. No answers or hidden pictures of the Statue of Liberty appeared from his staring into the middle distance.

In the past he had never been concerned with his age, and was more concerned with what his body could do than how it looked. But in the past few months he had been thinking more about the future, and wondering if he had wasted some of the years gone by. This morning he noticed the wrinkles forming around his eyes, rather than the blue-green irises. He also noticed the increased gray stubble that had shown up in his four-day beard.

He broke out of his reverie and left the cool air of the restroom. The sky was now completely clear, and the temperature seemed to have climbed a few degrees while he was inside. Fully fueled and relieved, he returned to his bike to continue his journey. It would be wise to get in some miles this morning before the temperatures climbed too high. There was still a long way to go, and several hills to climb.

III

Back out on the road, he tried to recapture some momentum. The first mile or two after a stop was always a little creaky while his muscles chased away the stiffness.

Michael was passing through what looked like farm country, with open fields and houses separated by acreage. Many of the fields looked empty, but he wasn't sure if this was an indication of weather, economy, or just part of the growing cycle. Like most Americans these days, he knew almost nothing about where the food on his plate came from.

In some areas, 101 looks more like a country road than a highway as it meanders down the coast, in and out of small towns. Most north-south traffic had moved inland to the straighter and faster Interstate 5, leaving 101 to history and local traffic. It is actually a designated bikeway through the state of Oregon, and he hoped that California drivers were used to seeing bikes sharing the road as well.

Towing the trailer definitely made riding more challenging. The weight of all his gear slowed him down, and the additional width made it more difficult for cars to pass. In one way, it made drivers more careful, and they gave him a wider berth than they typically would. On the flip side, if there was traffic coming the other way, they had to wait longer to pass.

At times their frustration was almost palpable enough to feel through the glass and steel. Mike did his best to be courteous, but took the lane when the lack of a shoulder made it necessary. So far he had run-ins with a few angry drivers, but fortunately their reactions had been limited to honking and hand gestures.

The two places where he felt the physical weight of the trailer the most were in the cities, and when the road tipped uphill. Normally, he loved to attack hills from the bottom, stand on the pedals and beat the hill into submission. Pulling the trailer, he had to accept a more steady pace up the inclines. He supposed there was nothing wrong with a little humility, but he still found himself pushing it now and then. The fits and starts of in-town traffic signals were the most frustrating, however, forcing him to stand on the pedals just to get moving from a dead stop.

But for the next hour or two, it looked like he would have a little biker heaven of flat, open roads with not a red light in sight. Even the cars seemed to have disappeared for a while. As his pace quickened and the caffeine started doing its thing, his thoughts picked up speed as well. Flashes of memory flew through his mind like random scenes in a movie. Each one was a little ice pick to the brain, and he actually felt himself flinch as they shot by.

He had grown up believing that he had to be strong at all times, to keep his head above the fray. He took to heart the opening line of *If* by Rudyard Kipling, "If you can keep your head when all about you are losing theirs and blaming it on you…"

In moments of crisis, someone has to be strong, and Mike had believed he was that guy. Emotions were flighty, flaky and unstable. Best to wall them off and let them out only when appropriate.

But after a time, there seemed to be fewer and fewer "appropriate" times. He built his wall and called it strength. Behind it he hid his emotions and oppressive feelings of failure. He was his own worst critic and would berate himself for the smallest of errors. What remained on the world's side of the wall was just a shell of who he was, like the shed skin of a snake.

A certain unspoken distance had developed between Mike and his friends, and quite frankly, he was surprised that some of them stuck around. Now here he was putting real miles between himself and the ones he loved, alone with the person he could stand the least. Himself.

Pressure was building and cracks were forming. Out here on a beautiful road, away from prying eyes or questions, maybe he should just let everything wash over him.

But he feared that once he pulled down one brick from his personal wall, there would be more than just a focused jet of water to deal with. All the bricks in the wall were relying on lateral tension, and if one was removed, they would all come tumbling down. The torrent of twenty years of emotion could not be tamed, and he would have to swim for his life until things reached some sort of equilibrium. And right now, it felt like he would still be under water when the cascade ceased.

So he scrambled around like a mad man, pushing back at the loosening bricks as leaks developed. Maybe if he picked one of them and eased it out just a bit, some tension would be released.

Amidst the onslaught of images that swirled around behind the wall, the one that kept picking at him this morning was the day they decided to have their first child.

IV

They had met through mutual friends at some party or another. He was initially drawn to the light he saw in her eyes. She seemed to radiate positive feeling, but did not step forward to take the center of the room. She seemed to perfectly balance the personality of a wallflower with the life of the party. She did nothing overt to draw attention to herself, but once you saw her, you could not look away.

They began dating shortly after the party. She actually asked for the first date. Mike had designs, but had not worked up the courage to pick up the phone yet. He had always been somewhat shy, particularly around women he found attractive.

It was not a whirlwind romance, but to Mike it seemed as if they were the perfect couple almost immediately. They fit together like a dovetail joint, their character traits interlacing with each other's empty spaces. Her smile and enthusiasm broke through his reserved shell, and he was a better man when she was around.

They didn't discuss it much, but they had both been hurt before. Both had given their heart away to someone unworthy, but this time it seemed completely different. They each floated carefully through the jagged debris of past relationships to find safe harbor. There was trust, there was hope, and there was love. There was no question in Michael's heart that he wanted to grow old with Katelyn.

They moved in together after six months, and there were no big surprises when they began living under the same roof. There was less passion than in past relationships, but Mike had chalked that up to age and maturity of the relationship.

And he also felt that passion comes partially from friction, and there was very little of that in their relationship. No squabbles about money, no complaints about their friends, and no petty arguments about emptying the dishwasher or changing the toilet paper roll. There were certainly differences of opinion, but voices were never raised, and no low blows were delivered. In his mind, they were married long before they walked down the aisle.

They were married on a beautiful fall afternoon, surrounded by friends and family. The day was perfect. The afternoon sun was broken up every so often by passing clouds, but it seemed to only add texture to the light.

The bride and groom had slept apart the night before the wedding, and when he saw Katelyn in her wedding dress for the first time, Michael was enraptured once again. It was the happiest week of his life. Not simply the day of the wedding, but all the days surrounding it. Friends and family flew in early, and the couple spent loud and quiet moments surrounded by the most important people in their lives.

It was a celebration like Mike had never experienced, and it reminded him how blessed his life had been up to that point. And it was only going to get better.

Shortly after the honeymoon, they moved from their little apartment to a rented house. It was an older place, and a bit run down, but it was in a popular neighborhood. They would never be able to afford to own a home there, but they could at least sneak in as renters.

They lived just north of the city, and not far from the University. The original houses in the neighborhood dated from the 1930's, but some had been torn down and replaced with multiple townhouses. Older residents lived next to young couples, and groups of students banded together to be able to afford living near school.

The owner of the house had no interest in putting any money into the house. He knew he would be able to rent it for the location alone, as long as it had four walls and a roof. The windows and doors stuck, plaster had fallen away in places, and it cost a fortune to heat in the winter time.

But it was all worth it to them. The neighborhood, the backyard, the walls unshared with loud neighbors, and the large, welcoming front porch. It was the first version of home.

The house they rented was only blocks from Ravenna Park, and Mike and Katelyn would go for walks in the evening, holding hands and talking about their days. The more popular Green Lake Park was only a few miles away but they rarely made the extra effort. Green Lake was always busy, but on those rare, sunny Seattle weekends, half the city converged on the park desperate to soak in the sun before it disappeared again. The quieter Ravenna Park seemed to be theirs alone.

It wasn't long before they got a dog to join them on their walks in the park. Though of course they were already married, the dog somehow added a further feeling of commitment. She was another source of love and another bit of nesting.

In another year they decided to buy a house. Prices were climbing rapidly, and they felt the time was right to take the next big step. They had to shop about ten miles north of the city to find something they could afford, but they were able to find a little rambler with a fenced-in backyard for the pooch. The house was old, though three decades more modern than their rental. It was dated but clean, and there were three bedrooms that they could grow into.

They seemed to be following the typical path to domesticity – marriage, dog, house – but they put off the decision about children. Most of their friends had settled down as well, and as the years went by, there were more and more children in the circle. Michael and Katelyn were the odd couple out, but they didn't feel any particular pressure to decide.

Mike in particular did not want to rush into things. Of course no one is really ready, but he did not want the decision made lightly. It was life they were talking about (or more accurately, not talking about). But as time passed, and they saw the joy that children brought to their friends' lives, the idea of children stopped being this hypothetical thing. They wanted a child of their own.

One spring afternoon they were sitting on their back patio, enjoying a glass of wine and watching the dog romp around on the grass. It was an unusually warm day before the Memorial Day weekend, and the sun shone through the maple tree, flickering diamonds of light on their faces. Michael turned to Katelyn and said, "So, kids…" Katelyn just smiled. They were ready.

Once they began trying, Mike went out and bought the children's bike trailer. He searched online and found a lightly used one in great condition. He stashed it away and was planning on surprising Katelyn.

It was sort of a symbol for him. Katelyn was more openly excited about children than he was. Though she had brought him out of his shell to a certain degree, he was still more reserved with his emotions. He wanted to wrap something up that showed her that he was excited too.

V

The route returned to the coast at Crescent City, and the change in scenery made him consider his progress.

This was day eight of the journey, and it was going to be one of his longer ones on the bike, roughly 85 miles between campsites. The morning had been quite pleasant, and the flat roads through the farmland had been a refreshing break. But the short trip inland merely cleansed the pallet and made the return to the coast spectacular once again.

The sounds and smells of the ocean soothed his soul like little else did. Like the warmth of the sun crawling across cool skin, he felt a feeling of peace wash over him whenever the ocean was in sight. Tension left his body from every pore, and even his heartbeat seemed to slow. Unfortunately, this return to the ocean was very brief and he was about to head inland once again.

He had never traveled this road before, but a friend had given him some advance scouting information a few years back. He had also used online mapping software to see what towns he would pass through, and more importantly how many hills he would have to climb. The morning had been blissfully flat, but the road was about to point skyward.

The first hill of the day was just south of Crescent City, and on paper it would be the most challenging so far on his trip. He would climb from sea level to 1,300 feet over just five miles. There had been plenty of hills, and even more on the horizon, but this one jumped out when he looked over the elevation profiles.

There had been the smallest ripples of elevation change in the first part of the day, but just outside of town it looked like he was about to ride into a vertical wall. He hoped it was just a trick of scale that made it look so menacing.

The day was heating up, so he did his best to take a sensible pace when he reached the base of the hill. So far he had been able to avoid the lowest gear, the "granny gear", and he wanted to keep that streak alive. Mike is a decent climber, but the added weight of the trailer made that granny gear look pretty tempting at times.

On past rides, he had talked to a number of bikers about how they approach hills. Most have little mental tricks to disassociate when they are struggling. Some count pedal strokes; some count breaths. Some sing songs in their head, while others actually plug into an MP3 player. Still others try to solve math problems or word puzzles to distract themselves. The strongest climbers seemed to have a short phrase or mantra that they chant internally to psyche themselves up to conquer the challenge.

But for Mike, his mind just went blank when he was pushing it to get up a hill. His mind was generally at ease when he was on his bike, but when he was really pressing, it was one of the few times where his mind went completely quiet. The focal point of his vision seemed to rest an inch behind his irises. He was disassociating in his own way, but there was no internal chatter. No stress, no guilt, no analysis – just white light, and maybe some stars if he was too far in the red.

On this trip, his mind went into these blackout periods more often. Not just when his body was overloaded, but also when his mind was similarly swamped. And it no longer felt like a mind quieted, but like a mind shut down, like a breaker trips when a circuit overloads. They had taken on the texture of alcohol induced blackouts, something he was also familiar with.

He hadn't put much thought into it before abruptly taking off, but several latent motivations rushed forward in that moment of decision that now had him eight days from home.

Part of it was the simple wanderlust of the road trip. He loved to drive and had always wanted to tour the United States. The original vision when he was a teenager was three guys in three cars, headed to California with no real plan. Later he talked about hitting the road for three months on a motorcycle. He would come back with great experiences, wonderful memories, and maybe some stories worthy of a book.

More recently he had dreamed of a bicycle ride across the U.S., but this trip was hardly the rambling route he had imagined. Though he was aiming for San Francisco, he was less headed toward something, than running away from everything.

He had also had this Thoreau-like vision of stepping away from the world for a while, stripping away all the chaff and getting to the heart of his own life. He had really been touched by the book Walden and had even made a trip back east to see the pond in person. But the vision of living alone in a cabin had been replaced with a future with a wife and kids. He imagined this step away from everything would do him good, but the trip did not start with the level of peace he had pictured.

But the thing that finally put him on the road after all these years was the desire for punishment. He wanted to beat himself up, feel some physical pain to match the sting of guilt he carried inside. And he thought this hill would do nicely in that regard.

Though he started off at a sensible pace, the desire for pain took over and he was now pounding the pedals like they were the cause of all his problems. Soon his legs were on fire, and he could hear his increasing heart rate pound in his eardrums. His breaths came in choking rasps, and his vision went swimmy. He crested the hill physically spent, drenched in sweat, but feeling a little cleaner inside.

When he reached what he thought was the top, it turned out to be a false summit, and there were some smaller undulating hills for the next few miles. The climbs were smaller and closer together so each trip downhill propelled him halfway up the next climb. His heart rate fell back to something normal and there were no longer stars in his eyes. Still he thought he might be hallucinating as he rounded a bend in the road.

Before him stood a fifty-foot tall Paul Bunyan with his faithful blue ox named Babe standing at his side. After blinking away some of the sweat that had poured into his eyes, he realized he had come upon another slice of Americana. In small towns across the country there were roadside attractions like the Big Ball of Twine or World's Largest Egg dotting the highways. Mike was now riding into the Trees of Mystery, and the latest tourist trap was a good excuse to take a break.

He waited for a pause in the oncoming traffic and then made a left turn to check out the statues of Paul and Babe. They loomed even larger as he approached, and the detail for a kitschy statue was quite good. Mr. Bunyan stood tall in his red flannel shirt, blue jeans and brown work boots. The statue caught him in mid-stride, and he was using his famous ax as a walking stick. His ox pal was a vision in sky blue and cloud white, and quite anatomically correct for a bull. A few laughing tourists were having their picture taken next to his undercarriage.

The kitsch factor was made complete by the person, hidden away somewhere, greeting the tourists over a loud speaker in Paul Bunyan's mouth. "Well, hello friend in the green shirt. Are you enjoying your visit to the Trees of Mystery?" There must have been some microphones nearby because the statue could respond to questions as well. Mike tried to stay out of the sightline of the voice of Paul, not wanting to get drawn in to talk to a statue. His sanity was already in question.

Closer to the road was another, much less cheesy statue. It was a copy of the *End of the Trail* statue, an Indian slumped over his horse with his lance-like spear pointed at the ground. This version appeared to have been carved out of the huge redwood stump on which it stood.

Mike saw a restaurant across the street, and he decided he had earned himself a non-fast food meal. The restaurant was a log cabin building (or at least had that façade), and the look was completed with a heavily pitched, green metal roof like those on mountain cabins and ranger stations.

He locked the bike to a railing and grabbed his backpack out of the trailer. With the guitar neck sticking out, he couldn't zip up or put a lock on the trailer flap. Of course, if someone wanted his tent and sleeping bag badly enough, a lock would do little to slow them down. All it would take is a semi-sharp knife to cut through the trailer's fabric walls.

He knew people with soft-top convertibles that left their car doors unlocked for this reason. It was often cheaper to replace what was stolen than to have someone cut through the top to get what they were after. He kept his few valuables in his backpack, so it was easy to take them with him whenever he stopped for any length of time.

Entering the restaurant, he discovered it tied in with the woodsy theme as well. Half of it was designed to look like you were eating somewhere in the forest. There were flowers and pine branches adorning the wall, and the stone floors were accented with heavy wood furniture. The other half was made to look like you were dining underwater. The ceiling was painted to look like water, and real boat bottoms and oars jutted down from the surface. There were even a few duck bottoms with paddling feet to complete the image.

He was letting his eyes adjust to the dark room and taking in all the decorations when a waitress sneaked in under his field of vision to greet him. He involuntarily jumped back a bit.

"Sorry to sneak up on you", she said.

"Oh, no problem. I was just taking in the room and zoned out for a bit."

"Table for one, or are you with a group?"

"Nope, just me today."

She led him to a table near a corner on the forest side of the restaurant. The cleats on the bottom of his shoes marked every step on the stone floor with a metallic click like he was wearing tap shoes. He guessed the waitress was somewhere between high school and college years in age, but everyone was looking kinda young these days.

She may have been older as it appeared she had been working in restaurants for quite some time. As she led him to his table, Mike watched her quickly scan each occupied table as if planning her next seven moves.

After they reached his table, he ordered a Coke and she dashed off to work the rest of the room. He just sat there for a moment, zoning out again. It felt good to sit on something wider than his bike seat, even if it was basically just a wood plank.

He opened the menu to find a wide variety of food, several with cute names to match the restaurant's outdoor theme. Often at the end of a hard ride, nothing sounds better than a big, fat bacon cheeseburger. But he had miles to go, and his stomach was still a bit flippy from pushing so hard up that hill, so he looked for something a bit lighter.

When she returned with the Coke, she appeared more relaxed and in control of the room. She may have still been really busy, but she had that gift of focusing in on her current customer in the midst of chaos.

"So, where are you riding to?"

"I'm shooting to make it to Trinidad before sundown. I'm making decent time so I couldn't pass up a nice lunch."

"Trinidad, huh? That is probably another 45 miles. Where did you start?"

"This morning? I started in Brookings, maybe ten miles over the state line in Oregon."

"This morning? Where did you start out from originally?"

"Seattle, actually."

Her eyes widened a bit as she spit out, "Seattle? How long have you been on the road?"

"Oh, it has been seven or eight days so far. I am actually headed down to San Francisco, but I'm not in a huge hurry. The scenery has been pretty amazing so far, so I am kinda taking my time."

"Well, you are headed into Redwood Country, so you may need to add a couple extra days. Why are you riding all the way to San Francisco from Seattle?"

Slightly lowering his voice for effect, he said, "Oh, you know, running from the law."

It was one of the many flip answers that he gave when people asked about his journey. When you walk into a room decked out in spandex and the day-glow colors of a bicyclist, it tends to make you stick out and start conversation. In a way it is a great ice-breaker and he appreciates people's interest in what he is doing. But at the same time he wasn't prepared to go too deeply into the motives for the trip. The flip answers usually bring a smile, and the understanding that he didn't want to go further.

He rarely enjoyed talking about himself, and had found it particularly distasteful this past week. He used humor and sarcasm as a defense mechanism, and their repeated use on this trip started to stand out. He realized they had crept into most of his conversations, even with those he was closest to. He was trying his best to act like a human being here at lunch, but the habit was hard to break.

He decided on a deli sandwich with a salad instead of fries. It was substantial without being a gut bomb that he might regret a few miles down the road. After the waitress ran off to put his order in, he pulled the packet of daily maps out from his backpack for something to read while he waited.

Each map had a bird's-eye view of the day's route as well as an elevation profile on the bottom. The experience of climbing the hill doesn't always jibe with what it looks like on paper, but it gave him a general idea of what each day looked like. There were a few more hills left for today, but none quite as steep as the one he had just crested.

He enjoyed the surprises he found along the way, but he couldn't leave the planning and organizing side of his personality entirely behind. His mind seemed to operate on a series of "what if" scenarios, and he liked having an idea of where the towns and services were just in case. It looked like today's route ended with a two mile downhill into camp, which was a nice treat to look forward to.

His lunch came more quickly than expected, and the waitress brought out a fresh glass of Coke, saving herself a trip later. The sandwich was surprisingly good, though now he sort of regretted not getting the fries.

With all the riding he had been doing, he felt like he was entitled to more calories along the way, but it was also a good opportunity to lose a few pounds. Weight loss was the cheapest way to improve your performance, and every pound he dropped would make the next hill easier. It didn't make much sense to spend money on the latest carbon fiber part to save a few hundred grams, when he still had several pounds to drop from his own frame.

He was used to eating by himself, and he usually just brought in a book or the newspaper to pass the time, but he found himself people watching more often lately. The intent of the trip was to step away from his life for a while, but he didn't want to drop out of society completely. He found he enjoyed just being around groups of people, if only as an outside observer.

It was probably after the peak tourist season, but the restaurant still seemed to be relatively busy. With the economy in deep recession, it was great to see any business doing well, if only for a day. There were several families enjoying their meals, and a few children had escaped from their parents' clutches and were running around the room. The tables were far enough apart that there was room for the kids to run without really disturbing the other diners. They giggled and screamed as they played an impromptu game of tag.

Ice pick.

His head twitched to the right and a flash of light behind his eyes made everything go white for a moment. His mouth went dry and everything in the room felt somehow heavier. He was glad he was nearly finished with his meal.

He caught the waitress's eye and made a check mark motion with his index finger. He wouldn't normally motion across the room like that, but he wanted to get out. Now.

When she returned, he paid in cash and threw his backpack over his shoulder with an eye on the door. Her direct look and smile halted his escape, however.

She said, "Well, I hope you have a great ride. It looks like the weather is supposed to be pretty good for the next week or so. Have you been through the Redwoods before?"

He stammered a bit, mind and eye on the door, "No, I haven't. I've driven from Washington to California a few times, but it has always been more of a straight shot down I-5."

"Well, you are in for a treat. I'm sure you have lots of trees up in Washington, but the Redwoods are really something special."

"Yeah, I'm looking forward to seeing them. And a bonus being on a bike, you're not flying by everything at 60 miles per hour."

"Well, take care, and watch out for those cars."

The conversation had eased the tension in his chest, and he no longer felt like sprinting, head down toward the door. He walked slowly and purposefully, back out to his bike and the safety of solitude.

VI

Everything was just where he left it on his bike. For the first few days he had tried to park his bike within his line of sight so he could keep tabs on it while he ate, but he hadn't had any issues so far, and he was getting more and more comfortable with leaving his bike unattended. He felt like he didn't have to keep looking over his shoulder for angry drivers or petty thieves. He hoped his trust would continue to be repaid.

Every time he hopped back onto the bike after an hour away, the bike seat took some getting used to. Somehow it always seemed a little harder and narrower than it was before. It took a little while to get his legs moving again as well, so he did his best to ease back into things slowly, especially on a full stomach.

There were a few more rolling hills, and then a glorious downhill back to sea level. You pay for these moments with the hard climb that precedes it, and the hard effort makes the reward that much sweeter.

The upper slope of this downhill nearly matched the intensity of the earlier climb, so he could have coasted to a pace above the speed limit, but he kept his hands on the brakes. He still didn't feel safe going all out while towing the trailer. He wasn't sure what it would take to roll the thing, but he had imagined the ugly aftermath more than once.

Halfway down the hill, the slope eased off enough so that he could just relax and lean into the contours of the road. These moments where he could coast effortlessly through the landscape were among the best parts of the day, and it was especially nice just after stopping for lunch.

At the waitress's mention of the Washington forests, and no pedaling to be done, he found himself recalling the day he set out.

~

He had left Seattle early on a Saturday morning. With all of the biking miles he was about to put in, he actually started his journey by boat. He took a ferry across Puget Sound to the city of Bremerton on the Olympic Peninsula. From there he would ride southwest toward the coast and Highway 101.

Less than a day of planning went into this trip, but he had accomplished quite a bit in that span of time. His computer was filled with multiple checklists from previous trips, and somewhat ironically, his past penchant for over-planning made the impulsive decision easier.

The first thing he did was drop off his bike at a local shop for a tune-up. He had done most of the maintenance work on his bike in the past, but a professional hand was probably a good idea before setting out on a thousand mile journey. And he had plenty of other things to do to prepare for the trip.

He scouted the route, printed up maps, dug out his equipment, packed everything in plastic bags, and tried to anticipate every contingency. He knew from experience that he would still get broadsided, but it didn't stop him from trying to plan away problems.

Once on the Seattle waterfront, he made some last minute adjustments to how things were loaded in the trailer. He was trying to get the center of gravity as low as possible. He had made a brief test run with it fully loaded the day before, but he still wasn't sure how the thing would handle with luggage instead of children.

He boarded the ferry around 7:30 AM, and after locking up his bike to one of the bars near the front of the ferry, he clomped noisily up the metal stairs in his bike shoes. The ferry was only half full, as the summer was nearly over and there were fewer festivals drawing people out this early on the weekends.

The main floor of the ferry had a cafeteria style restaurant for grabbing a mediocre but expensive meal on the run. It sat in the center of the ship, and around the perimeter of the deck were booths with plastic benches in a color scheme of a different decade. A few of them had tables, and those were usually snapped up quickly for laptops and card games. It was one of the few public places where Michael saw people pull out a deck of cards anymore.

Near the front and back of the ferry, there were rows of single seats bolted to the floor and connected by a metal beam. The seats faced the end of the ship and were either forward or rear-facing depending on which way the ferry was going. There was a pilot house and docking ramp on both ends of the ferry, meaning that bow and stern were only temporary designations.

On either end of the ferry, there was also a split walkway where you could step outside to watch where you were going or where you had been. He headed to the stern to watch the Seattle skyline slowly recede. He would eventually move to the front, but for now he wanted to look back.

The morning was cool, and there was a mist in the air. There always seemed to be moisture in the Seattle air whether it was raining or not. He leaned forward on the green steel railing and kicked his toe against the lower rail absentmindedly.

The prop wash from the ferry stretched out to the horizon like a jet contrail, or a dissipating trail of bread crumbs to lead him back home. West Seattle and Alki Beach drifted by the right side of his vision, though he stared directly eastward. He felt that if he didn't turn his head, the memory of the night at Alki could not creep into his head.

He focused in on a single point on the horizon and watched the buildings of the Seattle skyline get smaller and their definition blur. But the tunnel vision technique soon broke down and his mind was awash in visions of death and failure. Tears welled up as he watched the city recede, but he refused to let them fall. He rubbed his face as if he was trying to clear away morning cobwebs, getting rid of the evidence before anyone noticed.

His heart, already heavy in his chest, deadened by another fraction. With an audible sigh, he turned and walked toward the bow.

As he walked toward the front of the ferry, he looked out at the water through the side windows. By walking the same direction the boat was traveling, it looked like it was barely moving. When you walked in the opposite direction, it looked like the ferry was flying across the water at high speed. As kids, he and his brother would do laps around the ferry whenever their parents took them to the peninsula, marveling at how they could change the speed of the boat with their feet. He tried his best to focus on this happier memory.

Up at the bow he looked westward toward Bremerton still some 45 minutes away. At first glance, the horizon seemed to be made up of one continual forest. But as the ferry made its way slowly westward, inlets and islands defined themselves, stepping forward from the wall of evergreen. As the ferry skimmed across the water, he began to think about the road ahead. If all went well, he would make it 75 miles to the first of many campsites along his route.

Along with the bird's-eye view maps and elevation profiles he had printed out, he also had turn-by-turn directions called cue sheets that would help him find his way. He had created a little waterproof cue sheet holder from an old CD sleeve and attached it with a Velcro loop to the stem of his handlebars. He had a smart phone with all the GPS mapping bells and whistles, but these folded over cue sheets worked the best when out on the road.

A voice came over the loudspeaker and mumbled something about arriving in Bremerton. It always amazed him that loudspeaker technology had not advanced along with everything else. Announcements here and in airports were almost pointless as they just came out sounding like the wah-wah-wah of Charlie Brown's parents.

He headed back downstairs to the car deck in time to see the boat reach dock. Log pillars soaked in creosote stood in an open V shape to guide the ferry to the center ramp. Since there were engines on both ends of the ferry, the water below the bow was churned with prop wash as the ferry slowed. The captain eased the ferry into the dock with a gentle bump and the wood barriers creaked as they absorbed the final bit of energy. Michael's bike trip was about to begin.

Bicycles were let off the ferry first, but Mike pulled over as soon as he hit dry land. A biking friend had recommended some time ago to let all the cars off the ferry before hitting the road. That way you didn't have hundreds of cars (a literal boatload) trying to pass you in the first ten minutes.

The first day was one of the most difficult, but it had little to do with the route. There were plenty of hills, and they started almost immediately after getting off the ferry, but in comparison with other days, the elevation profile was pretty average. It was just that it was day one. He didn't have any days under his belt to build his confidence or stamina, and the first step is always the hardest.

As he crested one of the first hills and tried to shift into a different gear, he dropped his chain. The chain popped off of the front chain ring and his feet were suddenly spinning like some cartoon character running in place. The bike shoes have cleats that lock into the pedals for better power transfer, but you have to twist your foot to the side in order to release it. His feet were moving so quickly, and the bike so slowly, that he almost didn't clip out in time.

He had tipped over a couple of times with his feet locked to the pedals. It was usually more embarrassing than dangerous, but it could be really ugly if a biker tipped over into moving traffic. This early into the ride it just left him feeling like an amateur.

The route wound southeast along the hook end of the Hood Canal inlet. Here it was nice and flat, and he enjoyed a scenic respite before the road headed south and climbed once more. He briefly joined Highway 101 before veering off on a side road that paralleled a smaller highway. A ten mile stretch of chip seal pavement late in the day nearly broke his spirit and had him questioning his ability to complete even the first day of his journey.

Chip seal is a combination of asphalt and aggregate rock, and is much rougher than normal asphalt. Probably the only thing you would notice in a car is the increased noise, but the rough surface makes it hard to maintain your momentum on a bike.

This stretch of road seemed freshly paved, so none of the rock had been worn smooth. It felt like each sharp corner of the aggregate was grabbing onto his tires like a thousand little hands trying to slow him down. He pedaled harder and harder like he had something to prove this first day, but he didn't seem to go any faster.

But for all his first day struggles, he rolled into camp around 5:00 PM, and that boosted his confidence a bit. He would likely be on the road earlier on future days, so if he could make it into camp before dinner on this first day, he might just be up for the challenge after all.

From what he could tell by studying the maps, some of the campgrounds were near towns but others were more remote. This first one was in the town of Montesano, so he had more options for food on his first night.

He felt like he should eat in camp rather than in town the first night, to get the feel for life on the road. He stopped by a grocery store on the way through town and picked up a sandwich and a pasta dish from their deli counter. And a six pack of beer. No need to completely rough it.

VII

Leaving the grocery store, the road crested a hill above the town before heading back downhill to the campground. This meant his first pedal strokes the following morning would be uphill. This didn't seem entirely fair, but he would soon lose track of all the hills along the route, and stop attaching the idea of fairness to anything that happened.

He rode through the campground looking for a good place to put up his tent, and found a site on the bank of a slow river. The river was less important for camping these days, but the sound of it would be soothing. After setting up his tent and going through his gear, he sat down at the picnic table to have dinner and enjoy his beer.

Lately, camping had become less and less about roughing it. When he and his friends first started camping together, they banned watches because they wanted to be away from everything, including the ticking clock. But more and more gadgets had been creeping into their camping experience, and their cars and trucks were packed to the gills for a long weekend.

He supposed part of it was all the children now in the group, but the camping experience was becoming more and more posh for the adults as well. Gone were the hot dogs roasted over the fire, and now the meals were often better than what he ate at home. Some were even moving out of tents and into camping trailers and RVs.

Katelyn had not camped much before meeting Michael, but she seemed to take to it right away. She was thankful for any respite from her job, even if it meant sleeping in the woods. She also blended in nicely with Mike's friends and they often scheduled three or more camping trips over the summer. She slept in late most mornings, and Mike was happy to be in charge of all the cooking since she did most of it at home.

It was still great to get away with the group of friends, but as they added more and more stuff, it seemed to take away from the experience somehow. Tonight, alone here in Montesano, it reminded Mike of what it used to be like.

Along with his dinner and beer, he had a notebook opened on the picnic table. He had kept a journal in his twenties, but had fallen out of the habit of writing. He had found solace and peace in it before, and he was hoping to find it there again. At this early stage, he just needed to get things out of his head and down on paper. He would try to make sense of it all sometime later.

His normal camping gear included a big, three-burner Coleman stove that had been passed down from his parents. He loved how the ugly old thing still worked, and it was something that tied him to the camping in his youth. But it was left behind along with most of his normal camping equipment.

One of the few things he brought along besides a tent and sleeping bag was a camping percolator. He had resigned himself to simple, cold dinners, but he still held out hope for coffee brewed over a campfire.

Whether you needed it for cooking or not, camping just wasn't the same without a fire. When he was camping with friends, they would often stay up late into the night, drinking, talking and staring at the fire. Maybe it had something to do with the cover of darkness, or the intimacy of the fire, but it often inspired deeper than normal discussions.

When the Forest Service banned campfires outside of designated campgrounds a decade ago, it began the slippery slope away from roughing it. Gone were the days of bathing in the icy river every few days with eco-friendly soap. Now water flowed from a tap and many of the sites had showers. Lawn chairs and tree stumps were replaced by picnic tables, and fire was contained in concrete instead of being ringed by rocks fresh from the river. The paved sites in the state campgrounds felt less like you were out in the middle of nowhere, and more like you were camping in someone's backyard.

Soon there were fold out kitchens and blenders that plugged into a car's cigarette lighter. Margaritas were now served with the appetizers and cheese plates. Mike rarely showered while camping and still refused to wear a watch, but there seemed to be no fighting progress. Even by age 30, he was feeling like an old man longing for days gone by.

Though he was happy to keep camping simple again, he would not pass on the camp showers this time around. He would be just too dirty and sweaty from the road, and the synthetic bike clothing seemed to latch onto odors that natural fabrics would not. After finishing his dinner, he grabbed soap, a change of clothes and some quarters and headed off to find the showers.

The shower stalls were larger than standard ones and offered a tiny bench to put all his stuff on. Unfortunately, the bench was not outside the splash zone so it was difficult to keep his change of clothes dry. The showers offered three minutes of water for fifty cents, however there were no timers to tell him how close he was to running out of time.

Time ran out on him when he was still partially lathered so he had to pay for another round. He decided to use the remaining couple of minutes to soap up and rinse out his biking clothes. He had brought three sets of bike shorts and jerseys, so he could at least change into a set different from the day before and avoid putting on wet gear.

There was a brick fire pit with a built-in grill at his campsite, and after walking back out to the gate to buy a bundle of firewood, he built a small fire. He dragged the picnic table toward the fire and set the percolator on to boil. The beer was eventually replaced with decaf coffee and sunlight with a headlamp as he continued writing into the night.

.

VIII

He slept fitfully that first night. Nothing like the insomnia that had plagued him in the past, but he had been chasing a full night's rest for days.

The route on the second day was one of the few sections he had been down before. He had driven the same roads when he had a project in Long Beach a few years back. He didn't remember many hills along the way, but that didn't mean much.

The path a car glides over barely registers with the driver unless it is something special. All that is needed to cross a hill is a slight increase of pressure on a gas pedal. On a bike, every hill is felt. Every hill requires investment, and memories of struggle imprint more vividly on a deeper portion of the brain. But the elevation profile printed out for day two seemed to match his memory, so he didn't worry much about getting out of camp early.

He had never been a morning person, but with his recent battles with insomnia, sunrises were almost painful. Left to his own devices, and without the demands of a 9 to 5 society, he would probably sleep in until nine or ten o'clock each morning, and stay up past midnight each evening. When he was out in the woods and far away from an alarm clock, he usually just slept until the sun hit the tent and turned it into a sauna.

This morning he awoke unsure of the time, but did not get out of his sleeping bag right away. He stayed horizontal for a while and stared at the roof of the tent. He hovered in that state of low consciousness for a while, relaxed without drifting back to sleep. When he finally roused himself and looked at the clock, he was surprised to see that it was just past seven in the morning.

He unzipped his sleeping bag and rolled onto his hands and knees. It was clumsier than swinging your feet out of bed and onto the floor below, but it was about as graceful as he could manage while sleeping on the ground. The low tent did not allow him to stand upright, so in a crouch he gathered his clothes and toiletries before unzipping the tent and facing the day.

The sun was up but had not risen above the tree line, so the campsite was still bathed in softer twilight. As he rose to a standing position, he felt and could almost hear the protests of his back muscles. He arched his back and reached his hands toward the sky, striking a cartoonish waking-up pose that was nonetheless satisfying.

As he took his first steps toward the restroom, he felt how tight his leg muscles had grown overnight. He was restrained to short, choppy steps as the muscles that propelled him for 70 miles now resisted the simplest of movements.

But there were no sharp pains to speak of, and that qualified as good news. Tight muscles will usually loosen up if you start slow, but sharp pains are harder to work around. The softer elevation profile of day two should allow his body some extra time to adapt to the biking life.

He would not be showering in the mornings. It seemed a little silly when all he was going to do is get hot and sweaty within an hour or two, but he still missed having the warm water help him to wake up. Without a morning shower or a cup of coffee, his eyelids stood at half mast and his brow was reflexively knitted.

He splashed water on his face, brushed his teeth, put on deodorant and called that good enough to face the world. He decided not to change into his fresh biking clothes until he had broken camp, but he put on his sunscreen while his hands were still clean. He had brought along his water bottles and filled those up as well before heading back.

One benefit of traveling light was that it didn't take him long to take down the tent and pack up his trailer. He wasn't hurrying in any way, but he was probably packed up in under 15 minutes from start to finish. Since there were no people in the neighboring campsites, he didn't bother walking back to the restroom and just changed into his bike clothes standing next to his bike. He tossed the dirty clothes in the trailer, zipped everything up and walked his bike and trailer combo to the road.

Since he wanted to reduce the number of morning tasks, and because he was thinking more clearly in the evenings, he had done a thorough check of the bike before the sun went down. He pumped up the tires as well, so that once camp was packed up he would be ready to hit the road. He would continue to fine tune the routine in the coming days, but he was pretty happy that he was able to hit the road before 8 o'clock on the first morning.

Once he was back on pavement, he threw his leg over the top tube of the bike and pedaled toward the camp exit. The first few miles of any ride are some of the toughest, even when you aren't headed uphill. Your muscles are still cold, and the moment your butt hits the seat is usually a little painful. Those muscles in particular take some conditioning, and early in the season you spend the first few miles adjusting your position in a vain attempt to get comfortable. After some time your muscles either adapt, or your brain tunes things out, but there doesn't seem to be much you can do to speed up the process.

After the downhill coast into town, he picked up Highway 107, a two-lane road that connected the larger 12 and 101 highways, cutting the corner and avoiding the city of Aberdeen. Once on Highway 101, he would stay on this road for the most of the next 650 miles. But that was too large a number to think about right now. Today's route would travel another 78 miles and bring him to the southwest corner of Washington.

The first couple of hours were rolling hills through sparsely populated land. After passing by a lumberyard at the beginning of Highway 107, the roadside was dotted by far more trees than houses. The whizzing clicks of his coasting wheels reverberated off the wall of trees to become a dreamlike hum. He made slight shifts in pressure and weight and let his bike float back and forth below his body.

There are few machines like a bicycle, as simple as they are powerful. Little is hidden in the design. All the moving parts are visible, and you can trace the cables and chains to see how everything is connected. When you push this pedal, two gears and a chain spin the wheel forward. When you need to stop, a cable is pulled and a clamp grips the wheel. Every purpose, cause and effect, can be pointed to and understood.

Yet you are riding on the thinnest of lines, supported by something invisible. It is hard to understand how such a tiny portion of air could support your weight. In addition, the balance that keeps us from falling over is almost out of our control. It seems the more you try to concentrate on balance, the harder it is to stay upright.

There is something satisfying about self-propulsion, relying on nothing but yourself and the power of leverage and gearing. But as simple as the bicycle is, there are a couple of forces that have to be taken mostly on faith to make it all work.

After starting out slow, Mike found a comfortable pace as the sun rose higher in the sky. He reached South Bend midmorning, and kept his eye out for some place with coffee. Not far into town he spotted a bright blue building standing alone along the edge of Willapa Bay. If the bright, robin's egg color wasn't enough to catch his eye, the sign with four foot letters spelling out "Bakery" did the trick.

Mike needed no further convincing and pulled into the gravel parking lot. His front tire wobbled a bit on the shifting surface, but he kept his grip loose on the handlebars and didn't try to fight it.

The lobby was surprisingly small when he walked in the door. The room smelled of freshly baked goods, and the dusting of flour on the owner's apron confirmed that the majority of the building was taken up by a hidden kitchen. The glass case was stocked with a variety of tasty temptations, and front and center was a cinnamon roll bigger than his fist. Decision made.

There was no seating inside, but there was a three-riser set of bleachers bordering the parking lot. It seemed like an unusual place to have bleachers, but with the bay to your left and a quiet main street to the right, it was a nice enough place to have an outdoor breakfast. He took off his gloves and helmet, loosened the straps on his shoes, and settled into the moment. The coffee was nice and strong, though not quite as hot as he liked it, and the cinnamon roll was a heavenly combination of sugar and spice.

His diet had pretty much gone out the window lately. Even before the trip, more sugar and fat had found their way into what he had been eating. He found a little too much comfort in food, and lately he just stopped caring what it was doing to him.

And it cycled in on itself. The food made him feel good in the moment but crummy later. And when he felt down, he ate more. He hadn't completely lost control, but it never seemed all that far off. It felt a little more justified to be indulging while he was burning so many calories, but not by much.

Sufficiently caffeinated and carbo-loaded, he resumed his journey south. For the remainder of the day, the road traveled along the bay and was quite flat. Though he had no reason to hurry, his pace increased. After the chip seal and hills that challenged him the day before, he relished the smooth, flat roads this morning and found himself pushing the pace to see what he could maintain.

For a few hours, his brain shut down and he just let it all happen.

IX

Though he was hundreds of miles from home, and there were new sights around every corner, the evenings would become routine. Setting up camp, grabbing a shower, washing out his cycling clothes, walking around camp for a bit to loosen the legs, figuring out some sort of dinner, and settling in for a night of reading and writing. The mornings were a similar routine, only in reverse, and he found some comfort in the stability of the repetition.

He rose earlier than he ever did at home. Sleeping on the ground played its part, but he also found that he went to bed much earlier without the artificial light of their house and TV.

On the third morning he would be crossing into Oregon across the Astoria Bridge. The bridge is a four mile long span across the Columbia River which divides the two states. From what he had heard, there was often a strong crosswind to contend with, so it was one of a few things he was concerned with ahead of time.

The State Park he had stayed in overnight was at the southeastern tip of Washington State. The park covered some two thousand acres on a peninsula capped by Cape Disappointment. The campground was rather large in its own right, and his nearest neighbor was nowhere nearby. For now, he was enjoying the continued solitude. He was on the road early and ready to move on to the next state.

There was a back road out of the campground so he didn't have to retrace his steps back into town. The mileage wasn't much different, but it was satisfying on some level not having to backtrack. The road ran along the water's edge as it made its way east toward the bridge. A low haze of fog hovered over the river, clouding the view of the Oregon shore.

Within a few miles he came upon a tunnel cutting through a low hillside blocking the path east. Just shy of the tunnel entrance was a large yellow highway sign with the universal bike symbol. Above the peak of the yellow diamond was a hazard light, and below another sign read, "Bikes in tunnel when flashing. Speed 30."

Pulling over, he saw below the yellow sign was a much smaller sign that only a slower moving bike could read. It instructed bicyclists to push the button before entering the tunnel.

Mike looked ahead to the tunnel and saw that it was unlit and there was absolutely no shoulder. The eyes of drivers moving from daylight to the dark tunnel would not have time to adjust before they were right on top of a bike in the tunnel. It was a thoughtful nod to safety, and Mike hoped it hadn't taken an accident for the highway department to recognize the danger potential.

He hit what was essentially a crosswalk button and the light on top of the sign began flashing yellow. It would likely flash for a couple of minutes before going dark once again. He rode through the tunnel without incident.

Shortly after leaving the tunnel, he could see the Astoria Bridge off in the distance. The first portion was an elevated arch before the roadway fell back down to water level, and he could barely make out the accompanying rise on the other side. He did not see any flags on the bridge to indicate wind, but from here it looked to be a pretty calm morning.

When he reached the bridge there wasn't even a whisper of side wind, and he offered his thanks to the weather gods. However, he realized there wasn't any shoulder to speak of on the bridge deck, so the four mile journey still ended up being nerve-racking.

Somewhere around mid-span an RV blew by him, followed closely by an 18 wheel semi. It felt like their massive side mirrors had narrowly missed his head, and the wall of air the two house-sized vehicles pushed out of their way thrust his bike and trailer forward. The wave of wind seemed to pull the air out of his lungs on its way by, so he didn't even have the breath to voice the "Holy Shit!" in his mind.

His arms and back went stiff, and he struggled to get his wheel to follow the white line at the edge of the road. He was rattled and trapped, and the space between the concrete barrier and rush of vehicles seemed to shrink further. He could only make tiny corrections to avoid falling off the tightrope.

There was nowhere to pull off, so the only way out was forward. He pressed on toward the opposite shore two miles in the distance, keeping a nervous eye on the tiny rearview mirror attached to his helmet. He didn't want to be surprised by another wall of wind and steel.

The climb on the Oregon side of the bridge turned out to be long and steep, so the cars whipped by even faster as he slowed down. The road crested and then banked into a roundabout. He was thankful to be almost off the bridge, but the side of the road was littered with debris, and it made for a nervous descent as he weaved around the obstacles.

After reaching solid ground, he soft pedaled to allow his heart and head to calm down. A half mile later, he came to another long bridge with a sign indicating that this was the way to the Oregon Coast Bike Route. It was a much mellower crossing, and Mike hoped that it was a better indication of what the Oregon roads would be like.

Once into Oregon, Highway 101 turned south along the coast and Mike was treated to astounding views of the ocean for much of the day. He stopped at a deli in Cannon Beach for lunch. Afterward, he wandered across the street to an ice cream shop. He had to stop in for a cone in honor of Gerry who was his guide for this trip.

He had met Gerry a couple of years ago on a local group ride. It was one of the last club rides of the season, and the route circled the Kitsap Peninsula at a time when the fall leaves were in their multi-colored prime. It was a new ride for Mike, and once he stepped off the ferry from Edmonds, he looked around for some indication of where to go next. Recognizing the confused look on Mike's face, Gerry warmly greeted him and welcomed him to the Kitsap Color Classic.

Gerry had taken the same ferry to the peninsula, and he pulled over when he saw Mike with a map out. He had been on this ride before, so he led Mike on to the start line. They chatted amiably as bicyclists often do when meeting each other out on the road, and they ended up sticking together for the whole day.

They had both decided on the longer 64 mile route, and they got to know each other as their tires hummed along the pavement. Gerry actually lived on Whidbey Island to the north, and he often made this ride part of his fall schedule. He pointed out areas of interest along the way, and seemed to enjoy it as if it was his first time out.

Mike guessed Gerry was in his mid to late sixties, though it was always a little tough to tell a rider's age behind the helmet and wrap-around glasses. But the difference in their ages didn't seem to matter, and the conversation flowed easily. They chatted about every little thing - growing up in the area, the beauty of Washington in the fall, work, their families, and of course, all the bike rides they had done previously.

Each story led to another, and they found that they had shared the same road multiple times. Along with some smaller events, they both had done the century rides to Portland and Vancouver, Canada. They had probably ridden right by each other more than once, seeing but not seeing.

Gerry also talked about some larger multi-day and multi-week rides he had done. He had done the week-long Ride Around Washington, a route that changed each year to show off different parts of the state. He had also raised money for charity while biking down the west coast and even all the way across the country. He was particularly passionate about the fundraising rides and said they were experiences of a lifetime.

Gerry had not only seen the most beautiful parts of the state and country, but he had made some wonderful friends along the way as well. He had actually stayed the previous night with a friend he met on the Ride Across America, which is why he was on the same ferry as Mike this morning. When Mike expressed real interest in these big fundraising rides, Gerry could hardly contain his enthusiasm as story after story spilled out.

Gerry had this energy, this love of life that implied there was nothing he would rather be doing than spending time with you. Mike was particularly interested in the ride down the Pacific Coast as it was easier to imagine taking two weeks off rather than the seven weeks to ride across the country. He tried to steer the conversation in that direction, and Gerry was only too happy to oblige.

When they neared the end of the ride, Gerry said that they had to stop off somewhere first. They pulled up to an ice cream shop a block or two off the route. You wouldn't have known it was there if you followed the ride map, but Gerry clearly had some insider knowledge.

They dismounted, took off their helmets and glasses, and walked into a little shop that looked nothing like the major chains Mike was used to. No 31 flavors or gimmicks of mixing flavors on a granite counter top – just twelve or so flavors and impressive sized waffle cones made on the press behind the counter.

There was already a smile on Gerry's face, but it grew larger and he gave Michael a little wink as they approached the counter. There was twinkle in Gerry's eye that let you know he was smiling through to his soul. He radiated happiness, and the effect was as powerful as the sun they had just escaped. The effort of the day fell away from his face, and he looked years younger than the wisps of gray hair that stood at odd angles after being trapped under a helmet all day would indicate. Michael felt a smile spread across his face of its own volition.

There was no shout of "Gerry" like he was Norm from the TV show Cheers, but it was clear that he was in one of those home-

Sean Day

away-from-home places. Mike had his coffee shops; Gerry had his ice cream parlors. They took their double dip cones to the metal tables outside and sat back to enjoy the spoils of victory in the afternoon sun.

After talking about various things, Mike asked again about the bike trip down the Pacific Coast. "So, what are the days like? How far do you ride, and where do you stay?"

"I won't lie, the route is pretty hilly, but the scenery makes it all worthwhile. And the ride organizers take really good care of you. They haul your gear from campsite to campsite, and there are a couple of support stops along the route each day. Breakfasts are the typical bagel, banana and coffee thing that you see on most rides, but the dinners are top notch. They bring a couple of cooks along to prepare dinner in the campgrounds each night, and all you need to do is help clean up once in a while."

He continued, "You're camping, of course, but the campgrounds are decent, and I think there were showers at almost all of them. And don't be scared off by the fundraising. It's not as hard as it sounds."

"It sounds like a pretty spectacular ride, and all for a good cause."

Gerry smiled and said, "You'd have a hard time finding a more beautiful ride. The Oregon and California coasts are fantastic. You'd think it would get repetitive and one beach would look like another, but I guarantee you'd take hundreds of pictures and still feel like you missed something. It is one of those things you should do if you get the chance. I can get you copies of all the ride information if you want to take a look at it."

"Oh, that would be great. I am kind of working for myself these days, so it might be possible to get away for a couple of weeks. What time of year do they do the ride?"

"It is usually in the middle of September, right after school starts. Kids are back in school, so the campgrounds aren't as booked up. And the weather is still nice at that point."

"Well you've sold me. I would love any information you have on it."

48

They exchanged physical and e-mail addresses after finishing up their ice cream. True to his word, a week later Gerry mailed off a huge packet of maps, cue sheets, fundraising ideas, and even slipped in a couple of pictures to help seal the deal.

Gerry also invited Michael to an annual ride that he did with several of his biking pals in the spring. He organized a ride through the tulip fields in Skagit County when the flowers were in full bloom just before they are harvested.

Mike met up with Gerry and fifteen of his riding friends for the tulip ride the following April. The multi-colored fields of tulips were even more gorgeous than he had described. They found themselves pulling over several times to wander among the flowers, choosing places where cars couldn't park so they had the fields all to their own.

There were several nurseries along the way where the car folk could get out and tour, and the riders stopped there as well for hot cider. It was an extremely peaceful day, and Mike got to hear several more stories about Gerry and the multi-week rides from the other riders. Without prompting, they mentioned Gerry's love for ice cream shops and his ability to sniff them out. Not that there was any doubt, but the stories reinforced Mike's image of Gerry as a star that drew good things and good people into his orbit.

He stayed in contact with Gerry and even a couple of his riding buddies. They met up for some rides over the summer and fall, and he even ran into Gerry by chance at the next Seattle to Vancouver ride. But Mike was still struggling to get his business going, and the dream of doing any of the fundraising rides were put on the back burner.

Then the following winter, Gerry went into the hospital for what they thought was pneumonia. He had been feeling ill and just couldn't seem to kick whatever bug he had picked up. The chest pain increased to the point that he could no longer ignore it and went to see his doctor.

He was correct in his self-diagnosis of pneumonia, but it turned out that there was more going on. When his blood work came back it showed that he also had a type of leukemia. He never left the hospital and passed away a few days later.

When Michael heard the news, he was devastated. It was hard to imagine that this man who exuded life was now gone, and so quickly after being diagnosed. Mike had largely been spared the death of someone close to him. His grandparents had passed away, but he hadn't experienced the death of a friend before.

Even so, his reaction surprised him somewhat. After all, he had only seen Gerry in person a handful of times. But you didn't have to be around him long for Gerry to get into your heart. He found himself crying in Katelyn's arms when he got the e-mail.

There was a memorial about two weeks later, and Mike joined thirty of Gerry's biking friends to do a short ride together before the service. When they reached the church they found hundreds of people there to honor Gerry in their own way. Mike heard new and wonderful stories about Gerry, his life, and what he meant to his friends and family.

One of the stories at the memorial made a nice comparison of Gerry's riding style and his life. Gerry was never the first into camp at the end of the day. He was certainly a strong enough rider, he just wasn't in a hurry. He'd take his time enjoying the sights and the day, making several stops along the way - especially if there was an ice cream shop. For Gerry it was never about the destination, it was about the journey. No need to rush through it.

At the reception afterward, people from various parts of Gerry's life mingled together while a slide show of photos played in the background. There were smiles and chuckles as one story led to another, and an even clearer picture of the man was painted. And, of course, there were ice cream bars, custom made for the occasion by a local shop.

Over the next couple of days, Mike would pull out photos of their rides together. And he looked over all the Pacific Coast information Gerry had sent him after the first time they met. He reaffirmed to himself that he would one day do the fundraising ride. It would be a small way to honor Gerry's memory.

Unfortunately, things did not work out as planned, and he was unable to do the organized charity ride. But here he was on the route Gerry had described that first day, with the thick packet of information Gerry had sent him was his guide.

He also carried with him the pictures Gerry had thoughtfully tucked in the envelope. One was a picture of Gerry with his bike above his head near the Golden Gate Bridge. He had a huge smile on his face, and you could see the twinkle in his eye even in the photo. Mike also affixed a picture of Gerry and himself to his bike so he saw it every time he started out. Gerry was with him in spirit, and the pictures helped remind him that he always had company even when alone.

The pictures on the bike were a nice nod, but there was no better tribute to Gerry than stopping along the way for an ice cream cone. In Cannon Beach he raised the double dip cone to the sky as a toast, and thanked whatever power allowed their paths to cross, even for a short time.

X

Cannon Beach was a tourist destination without becoming a gaudy tourist trap. The little shops seemed delightfully local, though he was sure they survived primarily on outsiders. He meandered past the storefronts without going in, content to window shop outside with his ice cream cone.

It was just past noon, and he had time to linger, but he decided to move on anyway. He felt like he had seen the highlights, and it would take longer than he had to delve into the next level of the town. And according to his printed elevation profile, the 20 miles into camp were pretty hilly, so it would be best to keep moving. With the trailer and memories of Gerry safely in tow, he started heading south again.

Not far out of town as the road began to bend inland, the trees on the right disappeared to offer a great view of Haystack Rock. The massive rock sits just offshore along with a few smaller outcroppings. Of course, it is simply a rock; but with its location just out of reach, standing almost singularly against the immense backdrop of the Pacific Ocean, it inspires everyone to try to capture it on film.

For the first few days, he had a bit of tunnel vision as he rode. The chaos of his mind seemed to pull power from his system of sight, like his body was shutting down and only keeping the essential systems online. But as the days and miles passed by, he found his field of vision opened up a bit, and his dark thoughts were interrupted more often by the beautiful scenery passing by.

Though he hadn't been taking as many pictures as he might have on a more typical trip, Mike was bringing out the camera a bit more each day. With the advent of digital photography, the habit has been to shoot hundreds of photos to get the perfect shot, assuming that most would never be printed. He had a slightly different mindset this time around, and would bring his camera out only when something really caught his eye, and then for a single photo.

His memory of the elevation profile turned out to be accurate. The first ten miles out of town featured a number of rolling hills that were long enough to get his heart pumping again. These were followed by two much larger climbs that had to be conquered more patiently. He settled into a comfortable rhythm and just kept the pedals spinning.

"Just keep spinning, just keep spinning" started playing in his head, a takeoff on the "Just keep swimming" mantra of the cartoon fish in *Finding Nemo*. Being alone on the road, he felt more freedom to be silly without embarrassment, like singing along to the radio in a car. Of course you can get caught once in a while, and if someone saw him laughing as he rode up the hill, they might give him a wider berth.

After cresting the second of the two long hills, Mike was treated to a spectacular overlook of the Oregon Coast. The road bent to the left to continue on to Manzanita, but straight ahead there was a viewpoint where travelers could pull off the road and take in the view.

He was several hundred feet above the town and the coastline, and the day was clear enough that he could see some 20 miles down the coast. The hillside fell away sharply so he could see almost straight down, and the coastline bent left in toward town before angling right out to the horizon. It was a breathtaking view, all the more satisfying for the effort it took to reach.

He dismounted and rested his bike against the low stone wall. He extended his hands to the sky and tried to stretch the muscles of his entire body. When he stretched like this, it felt like he gained a few inches in height before shrinking back down to his very average five foot seven frame.

The view of the ocean was framed nicely by the few pine trees clinging to the slope below. Sunlight played off the crests and valleys of the water, and tiny bright flashes danced across the blue canvas. The deep blue was continuous until changing to a dramatic white as the waves neared the sandy shallows. The brushstrokes of white were much wider than expected, extending several hundred yards from shore, and not the single line of breaking surf he would have imagined.

There were several people sharing the overlook with Mike. Families with young children more interested in climbing on the wall than enjoying the view, and couples alternately handed their cameras to each other to get pictures of themselves with the view in the background. Mike offered to snap the pictures so the couples could be together in the photos, connected in memory.

He did not take them up on their offer to do the same for him though. He did not want to see his face on film right now. Eyes are the windows to the soul, and he did not want to gaze into them just yet.

Leaving the viewpoint and the people behind, he coasted down the wonderfully steep and slightly twisting road into town. Manzanita would be where he would spend the night, specifically at the state park south of town. He had arrived much earlier than expected, so he decided to hang out in town for a bit before going to the campground.

He found a restaurant with a small patio out back. He was able to wheel his bike and trailer around so that it was just on the other side of the patio railing. He could keep tabs on it and not worry about someone wandering off with his stuff. It had been a lovely day biking and reminiscing, and he was in the mood for a cocktail.

There was one other patron on the patio, who appeared to be a regular named Mitch from his banter with the waitress. After taking care of him, she came over and took Michael's order for a gin and tonic. Bourbon was Mike's more typical poison, but a gin and tonic seemed more appropriate for this sunny patio.

Though he wasn't terribly hungry, Mike looked over the appetizer menu to see if there was anything to tempt him. Maybe he would have a late snack, a second lunch as it were, and not have much of a dinner.

When the waitress returned with his drink, he ordered a combination plate of roasted garlic and baked brie that was served with some artisan bread. It sounded wonderful. Since he was largely alone on the patio, Mike made himself at home by loosening the Velcro straps and kicking off his shoes before taking a sip of the gin and tonic. As the gin entered his system, he closed his eyes and felt a warmth flow through him like he had returned to his childhood home.

Mike had been drinking more lately. What was once a weekend thing when hanging out with friends, or the occasional glass of wine with dinner, had become a nightly ritual. Over the past year, the occasional sip turned into two or three drinks each night. Katelyn would generally join him in a glass of wine, but less often when he turned to liquor.

He didn't drink to get drunk, he never missed a day of work, and a crowd hadn't gathered for an intervention. He told himself that he didn't have a drinking problem, but he was having more and more trouble saying that with any conviction. Though getting wasted was not the goal, there were definitely times when he had too much. He was losing control more often, and had even had a couple blackouts when he couldn't recall all that had happened the night before.

He was drinking nearly every day, and it was about as routine as his morning cup of coffee. He didn't think he was addicted, but it was hard to deny the place alcohol had taken in his life. He wasn't sure if he just *had a habit* or if he *had to have it*.

And he wasn't as sure that it wasn't affecting the other parts of his life. Were his synapses firing more slowly because of alcohol, or was that just the natural aging process? Was the drinking a symptom of depression, or a factor in causing it? Was it just something he enjoyed, or was he now depending on it for a place to hide? Were the blackouts and lapses in memory a sign of an overloaded mind or a permanently damaged one?

He started drinking more when he went to work in sales. He had switched careers when his previous job was eliminated through cutbacks and accepted a sales job thinking that it was the best chance for them to have kids. Once he was established, he would be able to work from home 95% of the time. Katelyn had a successful career and was now the primary bread-winner. For them to have kids, it made the most sense for her to keep her job, and for Mike to figure out a way to make money while staying home with the child.

But the move into sales had been difficult on many levels. He was not an extrovert so he knew it would be a challenging transition. But he believed in the product, and he thought that this would make it easier for him to be a champion of it. He hoped that his conviction would come across and allow him to make the sale without needing to resort to the fast talking banter and pushy tactics of the kind of salesman he hated.

Unfortunately, he chose an inopportune time to branch out into a new industry. He accepted the sales position only months before the recession hit in late 2007. At that point jobs were disappearing, and he figured he would have an even harder time finding different work. He felt that this was his best bet and decided to stick it out.

Before he would be able to work from home, he had to do a significant amount of travel in order to meet distributors and clients. The constant trips put a strain on their relationship, and the lack of money and stability delayed them from having children.

Though he spent a significant amount of time learning the product, and was able to explain the implications and benefits in great detail, he was unable to close enough sales. His salary was almost entirely commission, and his take home pay was less than half of what he made at his last job. He certainly would have moved on if there were other jobs available, and there wasn't the carrot to be able to work from home and take care of their child.

But now he felt trapped.

His failure to succeed weighed heavily on him. The feeling went beyond just doing poorly at his job. He felt like a complete failure. He wasn't even able to support himself at that point, much less provide for an expanding family. He had always been his worst critic, but the criticism grew to verbal self-abuse. He felt a physical weight in his chest and his stomach was a constant churning pit of acid.

Ironically, he would not have accepted this sort of abuse from anyone else. But the attacks were coming from within, and he was not able to put anything in perspective.

He avoided talking about work since he had nothing positive to say. As his depression grew, there was almost nothing he felt good enough about to share with friends, and he spoke to them less and less. The time he spent alone traveling for work made it that much easier to pull away. He slunk into his own little cave, safe from everyone's judgment but his own.

And in that cave, he drank.

XI

And here he was, sitting alone on a patio, drinking.

As much as he'd like to deny it, drinking and depression had a hold on him, though they were not the primary residents in his psyche. He had other demons in there now. Guilt, anguish, shock and anger clamored for attention and pushed any concerns about depression to the background. It is hard to worry about the foundation when the house is on fire.

His appetizer came and it was delightful. The full bulb of roasted garlic smelled powerful and smooth, and spread easily on the thick slices of bread. The baked brie was wonderfully rich without being overpowering.

He ordered another gin and tonic when the waitress came back to check on things. He smiled at the other patron (Mitch?), but his smile was repaid with a slightly disdainful look.

He had seen this look before when he was out in his bike gear. He wasn't sure if it was an anti-biker look, or simply a judgment of "what is an able-bodied man doing playing around on bike in the middle of an afternoon when he should be at work".

No matter. Mike was not exactly happy, but feeling a little better at that moment. He had not only biked across seventy miles of beautiful countryside, but had spent the past few hours cycling through some of the garbage floating through his mind. He did his best to shut off the swirl of thoughts for the moment, and just be completely present on the back patio. He ate slowly, trying to pick out distinct bits of flavor in each bite.

When the waitress came by some time later, he refused the offer of a third drink or a dinner menu. He felt like this was the perfect afternoon break, but he was ready to get into camp and set up for the night. After paying his check, he walked his little bike-train to the convenience store two blocks away. He grabbed a Coke, some energy bars and a bag of popped popcorn in case he got the munchies later.

All loaded up, he coasted downhill to the water before turning south toward the campground. After circling back after a missed turn, he found the entry road to Nehalem Bay State Park. Though there are certain staples of every campground, each has its own distinct feel. This one was the first he had seen with an airplane landing strip.

He had heard of people flying to remote Alaskan lakes to camp and fish, but it seemed odd here in Manzanita, a place easily reached by road. The buzz of an airplane seemed out of place in a simple campground next to the crashing surf. And when he pictured the pilot coming in low over the campground, landing, hopping out and putting up a tent, it just seemed absurd.

One common feature of the larger campgrounds was a separate hiker/biker section. The areas are a little more primitive than in the rest of the campground, so the sites are a little cheaper. The hiker/biker area of this campground was just an open, grass field on the east side of a dune separating it from the beach.

Mike had the pick of the place and decided to set up his tent away from the lavatories. He would have to be right up against it to use it as a wind-break, and he decided to brave the wind rather than be subjected to any wafting smells. There were no fire pits in this part of the campground, but that was not too surprising. Wind, fire and tall grass do not mix well.

The winds were actually pretty mild at that point, so he didn't have to struggle against them to set up his tent. His tent could make for a pretty good sail, so he did his best to anchor down the corners in case the winds picked up later. The tent stakes had little solid ground to brace against in the sandy soil, but he hammered them into the ground anyway, if only for show. He spread out his gear so that most of the weight was at the perimeter of the tent. This, and praying for calm weather, was about the best he could do.

After setting up camp and cleaning himself and his gear, he headed over the dune and down to the beach. He had traded his bike shoes for flip flops, and those were soon left behind when he reached the sand. It felt good to flex his weary feet in the sand, and he dug into the soft earth by twisting his ankles back and forth. The smells of the sea were somehow stronger now that he had the visual part of the scene to tie them to.

After a few deep breaths of the salt air, he dug himself out and wandered on to the water's edge. Without hesitation, he walked into the surf until it reached his thighs. The waves would occasionally send the water level above his waist sending a cold shock through his nether regions. He took a few steps back so the water was more at knee level.

He could think of no more relaxing a scene than legs in the ocean, toes in the sand, with the endless sights and sounds of the waves crashing onto shore. The cold water felt good on his sore legs and joints like an all-natural ice bath for muscle recovery.

He looked at the hill to his right and could see the viewpoint he had been at earlier, as well as the winding road he had taken into town. It was interesting to now be standing in the thing of beauty he had just been admiring a bit ago, and looking back to see more beauty in the opposite direction.

As he was apt to do when deep in thought and staring at the horizon, he placed his hands behind his head and interlaced his fingers. It was a mostly unconscious gesture like he was submitting himself to the vastness in front of him. He is not sure where the habit developed, but Katelyn had snapped a number of photos with him in that pose.

Several of the things he had been thinking about danced around the periphery of his thoughts, but none would take hold in his brain. The white noise of the waves seemed to prevent him from latching onto any specific image, and what he felt most in that moment was a certain tranquility he couldn't define.

He had always been drawn to water. Looking at a body of water was soothing for most, but Michael felt the compulsion to literally immerse himself in it. Returning to the water seemed somehow primal, and he felt like the liquid world could both embrace and wash away.

He recalled a quote from Isak Dineson that had resonated with him, and seem to sum up this moment, this trip.

"The cure for anything is saltwater – sweat, tears, or the sea."

Oh, how he hoped.

Back at the campsite, he did his best to settle in for the night in what was essentially an open field. The hiker/biker site was not only without any fire pits, but there were no picnic tables to be found either. He was not in a wooded area where he could hope to find a stump or downed tree to sit on, so he ended up sitting on the ground leaning up against his bike trailer. The grass covered dune was relatively soft with its sandy base, so it was a pretty comfortable alternative. He decided to pull out the guitar for the first time.

He still wasn't quite sure why he brought the guitar on the trip. There seems to be a whole category of things that get thrown in "just in case" when you end up with a little room left in your bag. Things that you probably won't end up getting to, but that seem sensible when you have all this free time ahead of you.

The guitar was also one of those things that had been sitting in a corner, silently mocking him with its lack of use. It fell in the growing category of things that he intended to do/learn/experience someday. Many garages are filled with weight benches, woodworking tools, scrapbooking kits and the like. Equipment for sports or hobbies purchased in an ambitious moment of intention, but that now only take up room and gather dust. For Mike it was the guitar.

He didn't know anything about guitars, but had always had this desire to play one tickling the back of his mind. He found this one in great condition at a garage sale a few years back. The fact that it looked brand new probably meant the current owner bought it and set it aside almost immediately, but this thought did not occur to Mike in time to question his own impulse.

He knew so little about guitars that he didn't even think to find out if this one was for a left or right-handed person (or if there even was such a thing). When he had played air guitar like any other imaginary rock star, he had always played as a left-hander. He was primarily right-handed, but there were a few things like dribbling a basketball that he did left-handed.

He liked the idea of being ambidextrous, having the freedom to attack things from either side. When he was younger, he even practiced writing left-handed, in case he ever lost the use of his right arm. His mind worked on sets of worst case scenarios and contingency plans, expecting the worse and hoping for the best. His writing with his left hand wasn't that much worse than with his right, but that wasn't saying much.

After taking his nearly new guitar home and looking for free lessons online, he figured out that this one was designed to be played right-handed. He held it both ways, and playing with his right didn't feel too awkward, but he wondered if he should just spend the money on a guitar for lefties.

He went through the first couple of lessons that he found online, which basically taught him how to hold the guitar and play two chords. And that is where his momentum stopped. According to the lesson, these two chords would let him (roughly) play a number of songs, but what he did didn't sound recognizable.

When he was packing up for the trip, he saw the guitar in the corner of the garage and wedged it into the trailer alongside the camping gear. There were so many unfinished things in his life right now; maybe he could tackle this one small thing. It seemed both stupid and profound to think that conquering one goal would have any effect on another, but he was willing to try anything.

He leaned back against the trailer in the fading light and strummed the guitar. Occasionally, he would attempt to finger those two chords from memory, but he mostly just moved his left hand randomly up and down the neck of the guitar to change the tone. He didn't really care about doing it correctly at this point. He found just the act of playing and the undefined notes to be relaxing.

He planned to pull out his notebook later to try to record his day and pin down some of his thoughts, but right now he was pretty pleased with the effect that the stop for a drink, the walk in the ocean, and guitar had on finishing the day.

He added a walk in the ocean to his daily routine wherever possible for the rest of the trip.

XII

He awoke early again the next day, but at least with a full night's sleep in the tank. The triad of relaxation techniques, coupled with the soothing sounds of the ocean nearby, allowed him to have one of the best nights of sleep he had had in quite some time. He had also set aside the notebook for a night, and just tried to appreciate the good moment without interrupting it with any analysis.

It was another 85 miles to his next stop in Lincoln City. He had been making good time so far, but he did not want to tempt the fates by leaving late in the morning. Weather, a mechanical issue or even a wrong turn could throw a wrench in the day. He preferred to allow some time for the unexpected.

The day's route headed inland initially, so he retraced his path through town before turning south. Without the splendor of the ocean to look at, and no coffee in his system, his mind drifted aimlessly for the first twenty miles or so. He could recall little of the first part of the route when he thought back on it later in the day.

This happened to him quite often back when he was commuting to his old 9 to 5 job. He would glaze over during his repetitive commute and the first half hour of the day was a complete blank. He supposed this was not unusual, and it is a wonder there aren't more accidents on the freeways.

He recalled one particular morning. When he started his car to go to work, there was a moth sitting on his windshield wiper. When he reached the freeway on-ramp a couple of miles later, the moth was still there. He wondered how long the moth would be able to hold on at freeway speeds. The moth's wings fluttered madly as the car's speed increased, but he managed to hold on as he merged into traffic.

When Mike reached his exit fifteen minutes later and stopped at the end of the off ramp, he realized the moth was still there. His mind had wandered and he had completely forgotten about the moth. His brain was so scattered that he wasn't even able to focus on something that was right in front of his face. When he started wondering how confused the moth must be, uprooted from his home by a hundred miles on a moth scale, he started questioning his sanity as well.

The miles flew by again this morning, and though his eyes were open, he didn't see much of anything. The miles just blended together, and he was left with only vague impressions. He was living too much in his head again so he tried to push his focus outward and pay attention to the distinct miles and moments as they passed by.

The cue sheet for the day had offered two route options, and Michael had opted to leave Highway 101 for the inland path. The road bent and twisted through forested land, offering filtered glimpses of the river it roughly paralleled. The road would bend in toward the river as if to occasionally check in on a child's progress before stepping back to let it wander on its own.

The trees were densely packed and jostled their way toward the road in search of open sunlight. They were thick enough to lower the temperature to the dew point and make it feel like he was riding through a refrigerated stretch of road. His jersey dripped with the gathered dew, and he shivered as the wind passed through it.

The road dipped and banked as it wound through the trees. The cant of the road was often in the opposite direction of the turn making it more difficult to navigate safely on the wet pavement. It was as if there had been no grading when they put the road in, and it just followed the natural contours of the land.

He saw a sign and learned that the road was named, "Miami Foley Road." The words seemed like a meaningless pairing, but they flowed together like a lilting tongue-twister, which he repeated in rapid succession. His inner dialogue broke through and he said aloud, "Miami Foley, Miami Foley, Miami Foley." It startled him to hear his own voice, especially in the quiet of the woods. It was the first time he had spoken of his own volition in days, outside of brief moments when he had to respond in order to get food.

The only town of any size along the route this morning was Tillamook (another pleasing word to say aloud), known for producing the brand of cheese and ice cream by the same name. His route passed right by the factory and visitor center on the north edge of town. According to the sign outside, there were tours 365 days a year. If he was further along in his day he might have been tempted to stop. If there had been a wine shop right next to the cheese tasting room, temptation may have beaten out prudence.

He kept going and headed toward the center of town for coffee and a late breakfast. He found an independent coffee shop that was fashioned as a cross between a library and an art studio. The room was dark and smelled of freshly roasted coffee, leather and old books. There were a couple of bookshelves and each had a sign welcoming customers to take and leave books. Paintings and pictures were scattered on the walls in an uneven, but pleasing fashion, each with a little card below with a price and the artist's name.

The gal behind the counter had short hair with a chunky cut to it, and the splash of red dye in her bangs provided a bright contrast to the otherwise black hair. She had a tiny hoop through her left nostril, a post through her eyebrow and a couple extra studs in each ear. Her warm smile was a contrast to the cool metal that covered her face.

Mike opted for an Americano this morning, a slight upgrade from his normal cup of coffee, mostly because he wanted to watch the barista work the older espresso machine. This was not one of the modern, push-button operations now found in the larger chains. He imagined gears, levers and steam driven pistons working in harmony to produce two ounces of the black elixir. She went through the motions with a practiced hand, all the while making the normal small talk to a coffee house stranger. He selected a banana nut muffin for breakfast that also bore little resemblance to its mass produced cousins.

Michael found himself chiming in to extend the conversation instead of heading straight for a table or the safety of outdoors. He lingered to ask questions about her, the shop, and the town.

"I love the look of this place. Are the paintings from local artists?" he asked.

"Yeah, they rotate out every month. New month, new artist, so the place looks a little different each time. Our regulars come in for coffee, books and the live music on Fridays, but it is mostly tourists that buy the paintings. Where are you from?"

"Up near Seattle. Down here on a little break. How about you? Did you grow up around here?"

"More or less. We moved here when I was in grade school. Right now I'm trying to save up some money before going to Oregon State. I just sold my car, so I am riding a bike these days as well," moving her eyes up and down to indicate she'd noticed Michael's biking clothes.

"Good for you. I haven't taken the plunge full time. I'm still just riding for fun at this point. It would be nice to not have a car payment, though."

"No kidding. Well enjoy your coffee and your ride."

"Thanks. You have a good day too." He headed over to an empty table and dropped his backpack onto one of the empty chairs. He set the muffin down on the table and wandered over to the bookshelves.

When he lost his last job and was considering what to do with his life, he had glanced over the idea of opening up some sort of business. There were franchise opportunities with a sub shop chain, and he had always had a soft spot in his mind for opening a coffee house.

He had spent hours and days in coffee houses during college, and it was still his home away from home. He could fall into a story and shut out the noise for hours at a time back then. It was a guilty pleasure he had never given up, and always relished an afternoon break with a book and a cup of coffee. When he pictured his own coffee house, it had a vibe similar to this one.

He was never without a book, and had brought a couple along with him on the trip. Recently, to save some money, he had been going to the library to borrow books instead of buying them.

But he missed walking through bookstores and reading the staff recommendations, or just letting a good book cover catch his eye. It was a brilliant move when bookstores added coffee shops to their floor plan, and he had spent many an afternoon wandering through the stacks with a good cup of coffee.

Michael enjoyed looking at bookshelves in people's houses as well, scanning them for new authors as well as forming a picture of the person from what they read. Here in the Tillamook coffeehouse, he lingered at the two bookshelves looking over the strange variety of titles. It was a manic collection ranging from sci-fi to romance, self-help to world history, pristine hardbacks to weathered paperbacks.

When he had hurriedly packed for the trip, he just grabbed a couple of titles off the shelf that caught his eye. His mind tended to kick into overdrive late at night, so he usually read in bed for an hour to quiet it down. He left behind the non-fiction, or anything else requiring much brain power. He opted for the mental candy of fiction heavy on plot and light on substance. It would have a better chance to draw him in, take him away. But he was still having a hard time concentrating and would reread a page over and over because his mind had drifted.

This morning he just glanced through the local paper rather than grabbing another book off the shelf. He had semi-intentionally avoided any news so far, but he missed the ritual of sitting down with the paper in the morning. This morning's stories were the same here as they were pretty much everywhere else – unemployment was high, houses were being foreclosed on, people were angry and stressed.

He still preferred the morning paper to the nightly news, though. Although the paper published stories of crime and tragedy, it didn't seem to subscribe to the philosophy of "if it bleeds, it leads" as much as the nightly news did.

And he still bought the paper rather than reading the news for free online. The primary reason was he didn't want to stare at a computer monitor any more than he had to, but there was also something comforting in the static nature of the newspaper. You can't go back to the web and expect to find the story you started but didn't finish an hour ago. The web page was constantly being updated with the latest development, and there seemed almost no structure to the thousands of links to other stories. The paper seemed to give him the time to read the details instead of merely chasing headlines.

The newspaper's once a day delivery of information also seemed to weed out much of the hyperbole that the 24 hour news networks used to capture the fleeting attention span of the public. Mike was all too happy to have heard about "Balloon Boy" only after the hoax was revealed.

After a relaxing break with the morning paper and coffee, it was about time to hit the road again. He set aside the paper and double-checked the next few steps in his route. According to Gerry's information, the route they had taken left Highway 101 again here in Tillamook to head out on a loop called the Three Capes Route. It added a few miles and several large climbs, but he was sure it would be a more scenic diversion.

He set out from the coffee shop, and was soon headed west toward the ocean. After a few miles through open country, the road bent north to join the southern edge of Tillamook Bay. For several miles, the road was no more than 20 feet from the water's edge, and meandered along the twists and turns of the coastline.

The road reached an intersection, and his route headed left and straight uphill. It was a jarring change, and after coming to a full stop at the intersection, he had no momentum to get him started. The scenery also changed abruptly from 180 degree views of the water to now being surrounded by an evergreen forest. The air was thick with a pine scent no dashboard tree could imitate.

The road climbed some five hundred feet over the next mile or two, and he was thankful that his breakfast had been light. The morning miles had been pretty easy and the coffee break had given his legs a bit of rest, so he powered up the hill as hard as he could. He was soon breathing heavily and sweating through his clothes in the cool shade of the trees.

Stars soon danced at the edge of his vision and any thoughts beyond the next pedal stroke fell away. He felt like he was reaching some altered state of consciousness that he had heard Native Americans used to seek through exhaustive physical challenges. He continued to strain against the pedals and the edge of revelation.

The road snaked right and left as it wound its way up the hill, so there was no knowing where the top was. In some ways the bends in the road were helpful on these long climbs because you weren't intimidated by seeing how far you had to go. The twists and turns broke the hill into manageable mental chunks. You just tried to make it to the next turn and hoped that it was the last. But then you had to manage the disappointment when it failed to reveal a summit.

He often kept an eye on the tree line because it helped him to judge how far it was to the summit. The trees seemed to thin in a certain way when you were getting close to the top. But this morning he just kept his eye on the white fog line at the edge of the road. Staring at the single ribbon of color, along with the exertion of the climb, added to the hypnotic feeling he was experiencing.

He rounded a turn to find the road had finally stopped climbing. It headed almost instantly downhill, but it was another false summit and he was soon climbing again. Thankfully, this hill was short as well, and soon he reached the true summit of the first hill of the day. He enjoyed a long, twisting descent back to sea level. The rush of wind over his sweaty body instantly chilled him.

He now understood why the Tour de France riders grabbed newspapers at the summits. After sweating their way up a climb, they stuck them inside their jerseys to block the wind and keep them warm during the quick descents. One more reason to keep the daily newspaper alive.

The road ended in a T intersection, forcing you to go left or right instead of plunging straight into the ocean. There were three large rocks before him, similar to Haystack Rock back in Cannon Beach, and after making the left turn he pulled over to the shoulder to enjoy the view.

The winds were still and the sun was no longer blocked by trees. He could feel the warmth seep into his skin a millimeter at time. A wave of satisfaction passed through him as he thought back on the climb. There are victories meaningless and small that still resonate. That and the warmth of the sun on his damp jersey sent a shiver through his body.

The route hugged the coastline, passing quickly through the town of Netarts before once again heading inland and uphill. The climb was only about half the size of the first one, and after a quick descent, it was followed by another hill almost exactly the same size. The Three Capes Route could easily go by the name of the Three Hills Route.

Heading inland under the shade of the tall pines, the air once again dipped to the dew point. Climbing in the cooler air was definitely easier, but moving in and out of the trees messed with his internal thermostat. Goosebumps rippled across his skin, only to be chased away when the trees opened up.

As he crested the third hill and started back down, the trees did not close back around him as had been the rhythm so far. Then he came upon a rather odd sight – there was a beach in the middle of the forest.

He pulled over to the side of the road and simply stared at the field of sand. It blanketed the ground like snow but in some strange world where sand fell from the sky instead. Although he had been seeing beaches and dunes of sand for days, he was far enough inland for this sight to be rather startling.

He continued to stare at the inland beach dotted by pine trees, but it didn't make any more sense for the staring. He supposed it was carried inland by the coastal winds, but it was hard to believe that the tons of sand that created this oasis could be carried in by simple winds. Maybe falling from the sky made more sense after all.

When he looked at a satellite map months later, he saw that the oasis was at the end of a trail of sand, like an inlet of water leading two miles in from the beach. It was still very impressive, but at least it made a little more sense. Standing in the middle of it without the perspective of distance, it was just dumbfounding.

The last ride downhill took him into the waterfront town of Pacific City. The calories of the muffin were long since burned off, so he stopped for a more substantial meal. Mike found a convenience store and bought a deli sandwich, a bag of chips and a drink. He walked across the street to eat his lunch along the beach. There was a hotel there, and he made himself comfortable on one of the benches along the boardwalk.

He was tempted to kick off his bike shoes and wander down to the water, but he didn't want to go through the hassle of cleaning the salt and sand off his feet. If he wasn't attentive, a tiny irritant like a grain of sand could go unnoticed until it had slowly carved out an open wound.

He unpacked his small lunch and spread it out on the bench. The winds had picked up a bit, and he had to pin down the open bag of chips with the bottle of Coke after it blew away a couple of times. He glanced away from the ocean and his gaze landed on his bike and trailer.

This was his fourth day on the road, and he was still kind of amazed about it all. Both by the distance traveled and that he had essentially stolen away in the middle of the night. This was certainly the farthest he had ever ridden his bike, and on past rides there was always a support car carrying his luggage. This time he was dragging everything behind him.

He focused his gaze on the trailer, stuff packed to its mesh walls and a guitar neck sticking absurdly out the top. And his mind drifted back to the child he bought it for.

XIII

After deciding that they were indeed going to have kids, the weight of making the yes/no decision seemed to be enough for a while. Katelyn was now in her mid thirties, so the clock was starting to tick a little louder, but they were still some years from the alarm going off. Michael was still traveling to meet with potential clients, so he was happy to wait until he was more settled into his working-from-home goal.

For Mike, the decision process of when to have a child was all too logical. He tried to remove emotion from most decisions, but it was a double-edged sword. By setting aside emotion and deciding things on the merits, it usually helped him to make a decision he was happy with in the long run.

But at the same time it could also strip away the joy and excitement of living in the moment and plunging ahead with passion. His habit of over-thinking was pretty entrenched, and he knew that it was something that Katelyn both admired and despised at the same time.

He had never imagined that he would be the stay-at-home parent, but because Katelyn's income was higher and more dependable, it simply made fiscal sense. They had also burned through much of their savings while Mike was trying to get clients, so in his mind there was simply no other way to make it happen. Logic!

But as their child moved from idea to reality in his mind, he became excited about the life they would have together. He began to picture the changes, challenges and joys of being a parent. Soon he could see the face of his young child in his mind, the perfect combination of Katelyn and himself. The button nose, the unruly hair, the off-center smile. He still planned to work from home and help out with finances, but he was already excited to take on the role of Mr. Mom.

After a few months of letting the idea of a child sink in, they sat down to talk about actually trying to get pregnant. Mike told Katelyn all he had been thinking about, and that it made the most sense for him to stay home. In typical fashion, he walked her through his thought process and let her know how he had arrived at his line of thinking. His tone and delivery were practical, and the excitement that had been building in his mind remained safely hidden.

Katelyn agreed that it made sense for Michael to stay home, at least initially. Although she was more openly excited about a baby, she was also proud of her career and knew she wanted to continue to work on some level. She had been thinking more stereotypically that she would be the parent at home for the first few years, but seemed okay with the role reversal. Her company had a generous six month maternity leave policy, and that made it easier for her to imagine going back to work sooner than she'd originally planned.

One of the things that they easily agreed on was that they wanted to have just one child. Although Mike had siblings that he really liked, when he envisioned a family of his own, there were always just three people in the picture.

Over the past few months, Katelyn had been doing a lot of reading about how to prepare for having a child. She had been taking prenatal vitamin supplements, and had done research into the timing of conception. She was really hoping for a girl, and she was convinced that there were certain things that they could do to increase their chances. Mike was happy to let her be in charge of all the details, but knew in his heart that they would have a boy.

They didn't get pregnant in the first few months, but Mike didn't read much into their difficulty. He assumed that it was a bit of a spin of the wheel whether or not you get pregnant, and that their age might make the odds a little longer. They just kept trying, knowing that eventually they would be blessed with a child.

~

His eyes refocused out of his head and back to the scene at the beach. He had finished his lunch while away in his head, so he got up to find a place to throw away the wrappers. He tucked the empty plastic bottle into one of the pockets in the back of his jersey, hoping to find a place to recycle it later. He stared at the ocean again for a long beat before walking his bike back out to the road.

A few minutes after leaving Pacific City, he was back onto Highway 101 heading south. The diversion along the Three Capes Route had been challenging but worth it. The difficult climbs fed a need, and he would have never seen the oasis in the middle of a forest traveling down the quicker path.

Although his life was certainly not a focused journey down a specific course, he rarely made time to wander off the path. He was more preoccupied with showing up on time, even if the next stop was not all that important. For once he wasn't interested in arriving anywhere, and could take the time to enjoy the journey.

Highway 101 was more heavily traveled and less scenic during this stretch, so his eyes wandered less. The shoulder of the road was wide enough that it was not particularly dangerous, but he still kept an eye on his rearview mirror to watch for approaching cars. It was unlikely that he would be able to make a last minute move to avoid an oncoming car, but he still felt a bit better if he paid attention to what was coming up from behind.

The road was relatively flat with a few bumps to break up the monotony. With his focus bouncing between the road ahead and the tiny view of what was behind, his speed increased. His pace seemed to increase naturally when his focus narrowed, and the first ten miles flew by in just over a half an hour. This pattern of flying through the boring parts in order to linger in the beauty became an unconscious rhythm.

He reached the base of the final climb of the day with good energy and plenty of daylight left. He had his punishing climbs earlier, and satisfied that he had beaten himself up sufficiently for the day, he took this last climb at a more reasonable pace.

The road widened to add a climbing lane. This was pretty typical on the steeper climbs, and Mike had come to appreciate it. The additional lane was for slower traffic, particularly the semi trucks heavily laden with goods. It was also populated with older cars that were past their prime, as well as the inexpensive cars whose engines were built for efficiency instead of power. The extra lane allowed the faster vehicles to get down the road without being trapped behind the ones struggling up and over the hill.

The extra lane was certainly not intended to benefit bicyclists, but Mike found it to be pretty helpful nonetheless. When traffic was lighter, most cars moved over into the left lane to give his bike and trailer a wide berth. When there were cars and trucks in both lanes, the ones in the climbing lane were typically going under the speed limit. It was definitely less intimidating to have a car go by at 45 miles per hour than at 65 or 70.

Late in the afternoon, he had the road mostly to himself. He was once again climbing into the tree line, and the protection of the forest and his slower speed meant there was less wind noise. He climbed in relative silence. When a car approached from behind, he could hear it long before he could see it, so he stopped focusing on the tiny viewpoint of the mirror. He fell into a comfortable rhythm and enjoyed the quiet between cars when all he heard was his own breathing.

There were many highlights that he could talk about when he went back home, but he knew it would be difficult to describe these seemingly nondescript moments that were still amazing. There were no pictures he could point to that would relay the sensations he found in the middle of nowhere. If he had traveled this road on a different day, or even at a different hour, he might not have felt them. They were born out of a combination of things coming together in that single moment, and were as much about his internal landscape as the scenery he rode by. He couldn't adequately describe it to himself, much less anyone else. He only hoped that he would remember it.

The road wound through slow bends as it climbed. Rounding one of the corners, he saw a familiar road sign in the distance. He had originally seen the sign on the back of Gerry's Pacific Coast Ride jersey, and it didn't make any sense at the time.

The yellow, diamond-shaped highway sign said, "Lane Ends, Merge Left." It seemed like such an strange thing to put on a commemorative jersey, but by traveling down the same path, he now understood why it was significant.

The route down the coast was filled with climb after climb, many on twisting roads so you could never be sure of where it ended. On the larger climbs along Highway 101, when a climbing lane was added for slower traffic, the additional lane ended at the summit. When you saw "Lane Ends, Merge Left," you knew the difficult part was almost over. It was the light at the end of the tunnel, so to speak.

Mike actually pulled off the shoulder to take a picture of the sign. When people looked at the photo, they would be as confused as he used to be. But now he understood why it was on Gerry's jersey, and it made him smile.

When he reached the summit a short while later, he crossed the street to take a picture of the small green sign that read "Elevation 752." All the pictures of shoreline vistas were beautiful, and might inspire a few oohs and ahhs back home, but the pictures of odd road signs would have special meaning to Mike.

The backside of the climb took him on another relaxing ride back down to sea level. The sun was making its way toward the horizon in the west, and as it shone through the trees on his right it created a strobe light effect on the shadowy road. Mike waved his left hand back and forth in front of his face, but the strobe effect wasn't as dramatic as he envisioned.

According to Gerry's information, the riders had only two days off during their two week trip. The first one was here in Lincoln City, Oregon and the second at Fort Bragg in California. Mike wasn't sure where, or even if he would be taking a day off, but he had decided to at least treat himself to a hotel room.

Lincoln City is one of the larger towns along the coast and attracts a number of tourists for the scenery and various festivals. Highway 101 runs through the center, and it is lined with hotels, restaurants, souvenir and kite shops. Most every business was crowded in along the highway clamoring for attention and dollars, so downtown was long and narrow like Main Street in an old west town. Mike rode to the southern end before turning back to choose a hotel.

He was more concerned with the location of the hotel than its level of comfort. He hoped to park his bike for the evening and be able to walk to wherever he needed to. And after sleeping on the ground for a few days, he was pretty sure any bed would be an improvement.

Highway 101 bent closest to the beach at a place where Devil's Lake emptied into the ocean. A sign on the bridge named the "D River" as the shortest river in the world. From what he could see, it wasn't more than a few hundred feet in length, depending on how high the tide was.

Mike looked more closely at places in this part of town but didn't want to pay for a hotel right on the ocean. There were no real chain hotels here, so it wasn't as easy to classify them from the street. Many of them looked to have been there for quite some time with only minimal upkeep, weather worn by sun and windblown sand.

They continued to stay open, so they were either nicer on the inside, or there were enough tourists coming through town that they couldn't be picky about which accommodations were still available. Like other off-brand hotels in smaller towns, a switch on the neon "No" on the vacancy sign let you know if there were rooms available or not.

Mike picked a motel within walking distance of the shops and that didn't look like it was going to fall down in the next couple of days. It was also one of the places that had some sort of pricing indicated on the sign outside. He did not want to go through the hassle and vague embarrassment of going into multiple hotels to see if he could afford it or not. He didn't have a specific budget in mind for the trip, but tried to save money wherever possible.

He pulled his bike to a stop under the rain shelter by the front door. Before dismounting, he stood up and arched his back to try to reverse the bent-over hump. His heel clipped the top tube as he swung a tired leg over it, and he stumbled a bit to regain his balance. He made a final hop and thrust his hands in the air like he had stuck the landing of a gym routine. It made him chuckle, but then he looked around to make sure no one else saw it. He hung his helmet over his handlebars and ran his fingers through his hair before walking into the lobby.

It was a smaller room, with an industrial coffee maker in the corner and a couple of newspapers spread out across a nearby table. The woman behind the counter was in her 50's, and she had a matronly flair without seeming particularly old. She was good at pleasant if superficial conversation – interested in your day without pressing for anything personal. She did not follow up with any questions when Mike did not fill out the vehicle section of the check in form.

She handed him a key attached to a plastic tag that let him know what room he was in. The diamond-shaped fob also had the name of the hotel and a promise of postage if it was dropped in a mailbox. You didn't see these tags much anymore, or metal keys for that matter.

Most hotels had disposable credit card style keys without room numbers listed on them. This was done both for the protection of the guest in case the key was left out somewhere, and to allow guests to check out without a trip to the office. But, of course, it also added millions of plastic cards to the waste stream.

Mike wheeled his bike and trailer around the building to his assigned room. He had requested a first floor room to avoid having to carry his stuff up any stairs. The woman indicated that they had plenty of available rooms, so it wasn't an issue. The room was not unusually small, but the bike and trailer combo was rather unwieldy. He had to disconnect them from each other to avoid completely blocking off the way to the bathroom.

The room was dated but clean. The bed had a brightly colored bedspread in hues of red and blue that somehow screamed hotel, though he couldn't say exactly why. There was a Bible in the bedside drawer, and the 21 inch TV was bolted to the top of a low dresser. The sink and mirror faced the front door, and there was a 4 cup coffee maker on the counter with packets of grounds and powdered creamer. It was like any other generic hotel room, with only the artwork indicating that you were near the beach instead of in the heartlands of America.

He pulled out his bag of clothes and threw it on the bed. His backpack with his notebook and laptop went on the single chair, and his toiletry kit was tossed onto the counter by the sink. It felt nice to spread out a bit in a space larger than a tent. And taking a shower without the need for quarters was going to be pretty sweet.

Though he wasn't paying by the minute, he didn't spend much extra time in the shower. His habit of a quick shower was so ingrained, he was in and out in five minutes. But he did appreciate that the water was quite a bit hotter than what he had in the campsites. When you were paying in three minute blocks, there wasn't much time to let the water warm up, and it didn't get all that hot by the end of the shower anyway. He spent a full minute letting the hot water massage his sore back.

He took advantage of the relatively endless hot water to shave for the first time since he left Seattle. He thought he looked pretty good with a beard, and sometimes grew one over the winter. It was some sort of nod to the season of hibernation, and he briefly considered keeping it for the trip as some sort of symbol of his step away from society.

But the thought did not last long. It was hard enough to feel clean while he was on the road, and the itchiness of the beard didn't help the situation any. It was also much easier to apply sunscreen to a clean shaven face.

Feeling cleaner than he had in days, and dressed in some of his few non-biking clothes, he decided to go for a walk around town. He hoisted his backpack onto his left shoulder, grabbed the hotel key and headed out the door to see what he could find.

XIV

He wasn't all that hungry yet, so he figured he'd walk around a bit to stretch out his legs and to see what the town had to offer. He headed north because it seemed that most of the shops and services had been on the road into town.

The winds were up and the sky over the beach was dotted with kites. Some of them rose high into the sky on increasingly long tethers, while others dived and dipped low to the horizon. These low fliers were controlled by two handles and multiple strings, and Mike thought they were called something like fighting kites. The sudden turns, spins and dives were cool to watch, and he could see how it mimicked fighter planes on an insane scale.

Though the wind was up, the sun was still high enough in the sky to fight off the wind chill factor for now. He had been exposed to wind for much of his trip, and it was getting only slightly easier to tune out.

Wind was probably his least favorite weather phenomenon, on or off the bike. It was just so random. Rain and snow were hurdles to cross, but with the correct clothing their effects diminished and they could largely be tuned out. Wind and its erratic nature was always screwing with you and demanding attention.

As a younger man, he had worked outside in construction, and it was extremely frustrating to work in the wind. It flung dust and dirt into his eyes, turned the plywood he was carrying into a sail, and made it almost impossible to leave any plans or paperwork out for reference.

On a bicycle, winds can turn your ride into a struggle. When fighting a headwind, it feels like you are perpetually riding uphill, and additional effort does not seem to translate to an increase in speed. It would seem that the odds were about even that you would have a tailwind assisting you along, but it never seemed to work out that way.

The most difficult thing on this trip though were the side winds. The onshore winds pressed almost constantly at his right shoulder as he made his way down the coast. Even the winds from the side seemed to slow him down somehow.

When the wind was somewhat constant, he found himself leaning into the wind, so he rode down the road with a sideways cant. But there had been a few times where a sudden gust came up and he was picked up and pushed sideways. It was nerve wracking to be tossed so easily, especially when there were cars passing by just a few feet to the left.

He often dreamed of a house on the water, but as much as he loved the ocean, he didn't think he could put up with the perpetual winds. Winds that brought sand into the house no matter how well it was sealed, and that forced you to push back just to stay upright. The beauty of the ocean seemed to bring with it the necessity of struggle.

Turning away from the ocean, he continued walking north. He passed by other hotels, movie rental stores, kite shops and knickknack stores geared toward the tourist traffic. There was also a Laundromat that he had missed on his initial ride through town. Similar to his appreciation of a real shower, it would be nice to clean his clothes properly after rinsing them out in a sink for the past few days. Maybe he could do a load of laundry after dinner or early tomorrow morning. Heck, maybe he would just stay in town tomorrow.

There were a number of restaurants to choose from, and like the hotels, there were no national chains to speak of. He had his pick of pizza, Chinese, seafood, and general meat and potato offerings he guessed would be classified as American cuisine. A sit-down meal with menus you held in your hand rather than read off a wall sounded pretty good right now. He kept walking to see if he came across a new find, and to let the ones he had seen jockey for his stomach's attention.

He ducked into a coffee house for a moment to sit down on one of their comfy chairs. He didn't want a cup of coffee, but it dawned on him that he hadn't checked the weather forecast in the past few days. He sank into the green leather club chair and unzipped his backpack to dig out his phone.

He had kept his phone off so far, both to save the battery and to avoid any calls or e-mails directed his way. The phone was actually set to airplane mode so he could maintain his moving bubble of disconnection even when it was turned on.

He powered up the Smartphone, turned on the antenna, and waited for it to find a signal. He had adjusted the e-mail settings to manual so that even when he connected to the network, he would not be bombarded with hundreds of questioning e-mails. He just wanted to be left alone right now.

Once it was powered up and connected to the network, he opened the web browser to check the weather. He looked at the seven day forecast, and it looked like there was a speed bump on the horizon. There was a brief storm headed his way, and some wind and rain in his future. After getting the disappointing news, he turned the phone back off and put it away, likely for another few days.

Back out on the street, he continued his walkabout north. There were a few other people walking along the sidewalks, stopping occasionally to peek in the windows of shops, deciding whether they wanted to commit to entering. School was back in session, so the tourists were closer to retirement age than the groups that likely filled the town during summer break.

Mike wondered how some of these shops made it through the winter each year. Did they make enough during the height of the season to be able to coast through the winter, or did the shop owners have other jobs to supplement their income. It was the same question he asked when he passed by an ice cream shop in Seattle.

He reached a point in his walk where the shops and restaurants seemed to be repeating. Another souvenir shop that looked like it stocked the same stuff, and another pizza joint with only a slightly different menu. He crossed the street at the next intersection and started heading back. The walk had been relaxing but had also boosted his appetite. He was ready to decide on dinner. He would stop at a convenience store for road food later, but it was time for a meal with silverware.

He decided on one of the seafood restaurants he had seen earlier on his walk. It had a menu posted outside, and there were a couple of things that sounded good. To be honest, at that point he wasn't all that hard to please.

He walked into the lobby and stood by the empty hostess podium. Not surprisingly, the restaurant was decorated with a nautical theme. Along the walls half cut logs stretched from the floor and heavy ropes were draped from the ceiling, and the occasional cleat and porthole completed the fresh-from-the-pier seafood theme. There was an L-shaped bar with a heavily shellacked top and bordered by more weathered rope. The decorations were several steps beyond subtle, but a couple short of cheesy.

The lighting was dim enough to provide intimacy without making it feel like a cave. There were a few patrons at the bar, and only a few of the twenty tables in the dining room appeared to be occupied.

Within a minute, a young and attractive woman approached. She didn't bother to ask if Mike had a reservation since there was plenty of room regardless. She led him to a table for two along the right wall of the restaurant, offered him a menu and wine list, then left to go get him some water to start with. There was a candle flickering behind hurricane glass on the table that provided some ambiance if not much light.

He opened the menu and waited for the words to clarify as his eyes continued to adjust to the darkened room. He had avoided glasses up to this point in his life, but it was getting more difficult for him to see at night. It seemed that the printing on menus kept getting smaller, along with waist measurements in pants these days.

The woman returned with the water, and it turned out she was the waitress as well as hostess. Now that he looked, the only other person out on the floor seemed to be the bartender, which he supposed wasn't too surprising on a mid-week evening for a restaurant this size. He ordered a Jack and Coke but hung on to the wine menu in case he decided on a glass to go with dinner.

The dinner menu featured several staples of a seafood restaurant along with a few local favorites. He was not a huge seafood fan, but the sea air had seeped into his psyche sufficiently to alter his tastes a bit. He decided on halibut braised with a wasabi ginger marinade and topped with crushed cashews.

The waitress returned with his cocktail and took his order. She had that certain energy of youth that infused whatever she did. She smiled and held eye contact enough to make most men delude themselves into thinking that she was flirting. It did not seem forced, which made it that much more appealing. It was that perfect combination of flirt and girl next door that had attracted Michael to Katelyn.

The waitress recommended a spinach salad that would go nicely with the entrée Mike had chosen, and he did not resist. She was soon off to put in his order and tend to her other tables. As Mike watched her walk away, he realized how much he missed Katelyn. He wanted to talk to her, but knew that now was not the right time. He opened up his backpack to see what he had to occupy his mind while he dined alone, and decided to pull out his notebook to do some more writing.

The notebook ended up largely ignored during dinner as it felt slightly awkward in the vaguely formal dining area. He was probably also a little embarrassed to have the waitress see him writing down his "all important thoughts." He simply wrote down a few key phrases that he hoped would get the ball rolling later on.

The spinach salad was as good as she promised, and the ginger wasabi was a flavorful combination on the somewhat blank canvas of the halibut. Though he was more of a red wine drinker, and did not concern himself much with wine pairings, he chose an Oregon

Viognier to go with his seafood. The flavors of the wine were round and deep and it held up well against the spice of the meal. He declined the offer of a desert menu. He was satisfied without feeling full, and he didn't want to spoil it.

He wasn't quite ready to go back to the hotel though, so after paying his bill he walked into the bar for an after dinner drink. There were still plenty of seats at the bar, so he put his backpack on one barstool and took the one next to it for himself. He still had his notebook out and put that on the bar in front of the backpack.

"What can I get for you?" the bartender asked after finishing up his conversation with one of his other customers.

"I'll take a B-52 on the rocks and a cup of coffee."

"You don't like them together," he asked a little puzzled.

"Nah, I like my coffee un-adulterated, but I like combinations of liquors in a B-52 coffee."

"You sure you don't want me to bring three separate shots of Kahlúa, Baileys and Grand Marnier?" The bartender was in his thirties and was already good at reading his customers. He sensed he could get away with busting Mike's chops a bit without worrying about his tip.

"Alright, alright, take it easy," Mike said smiling.

"Just checking."

The bartender tossed down a paper coaster with a logo of a local brewer as he left to go make the drink. He turned away as he released the coaster, but with a practiced hand it skidded to a stop right in front of his guest.

Mike looked at himself in the mirror behind the bar, his reflection partially obscured by the display of liquor bottles. His face had a little more color than usual, a combination of windburn and suntan. His eyes looked even more tired than he felt.

The bartender returned with the cocktail but not the coffee. "The coffee was pretty thick, so another pot is brewing. Should be done in a couple more minutes."

"No problem. I'm happy to wait for a fresh pot."

The bartender went off to check on his other two guests. He chatted with them amiably and asked them if they needed another drink by simply pointing to their glass. He brought over the coffee five minutes later.

"What's with the notebook? You look a little old for homework."

"I'm a restaurant critic. You're doing great by the way."

"Yeah, I'm not buying that. You don't dress the part, and you're not nearly uptight enough."

"Busted. The notebook is part travel journal, part Dear Diary, part great American novel. I'm riding down the coast for a couple of weeks, and my memory isn't what it used to be. I figured I'd better write some stuff down to go with the pictures I'm taking."

"Sounds like a fun trip. How far south are you headed?"

"The plan is to arrive in San Francisco in another week and a half."

"Wow! You are taking your time."

"Actually, I am riding a bicycle, so two weeks from Seattle to San Francisco is probably a pretty decent pace for the trip."

"You're riding your bike for two weeks?" Then he paused for a long beat as he looked a little closer at Mike. "Mid-life crisis?"

"Something like that." Mike responded with a resigned grin.

"Well, good on ya. A ride down the coast sounds less expensive than a Porsche or an affair."

"Amen to that," Mike said raising his glass in a mock toast.

The bartender walked back down to the other end of the bar to pour a couple glasses of wine for the waitress. Mike set down his cocktail and placed the cup of coffee directly under his nose. It smelled like a strong brew and it felt like he was getting a small caffeine contact high. When he took a sip, the coffee tasted as good as it smelled. With coffee houses on every corner, he noticed that coffee served in restaurants had improved. Even fast-food joints were serving name brand coffee these days to compete for dining dollars.

He missed human contact, but Mike did not linger over his coffee and after dinner drink. The direction of the conversation was moving too close to stuff he wasn't ready to talk about. Bartenders were reputed to be part psychiatrist, listening to the ailments of the customers on the other side of the bar, but Mike wasn't ready to dish about the stuff in his head or notebook.

He could probably steer the conversation to safer territory, but it just seemed like too much work tonight. He was only staying for one drink, so he just figured he'd quit while he was ahead conversationally.

He left cash on the counter and gave the bartender a wave before he could come back and engage. Mike turned, caught the waitress's eye and smiled a thank you to her before walking back out to the street.

Mike wasn't really anti-social, but he was just never quite at ease around people. It took a long time for him to come out of his shell, and he often leaned on alcohol as a social lubricant. But it only worked so well, and he hated going to parties where the only person he would know was his wife.

He had read that being able to go to a movie or out to dinner by yourself was a sign of a strong, confident personality, but at times it felt quite the opposite to Mike. He was able to be alone without feeling lonely, and that level of comfort prevented him from challenging himself to meet new people, or connect more closely with people he already knew. He was probably a little too comfortable being alone.

He knew he was building this up too much in his mind, and that other people were not much happier or successful than he was, but he still felt claustrophobic in new situations. He was glad to be back outside.

He wandered south back toward the hotel. It was still early in the evening, so he decided to swing by the Laundromat to see how late they were open. It turned out they were open for another two hours so he hustled back to his room to grab his pile of clothes. He dumped out all the stuff in his backpack and stuffed in the dirty clothes. He decided to ride his bike back to save some time because he thought he might be pushing it a bit to get his clothes cleaned before closing time.

The Laundromat was pretty quiet when he walked in. There were only two other people there, and they barely raised their gazes when he walked through the door. He went to the vending machine to buy a little box of detergent and exchanged his bills for coins to use in the washing machine.

After he started his tiny load, he settled into one of the beige plastic chairs and began to write. Hanging out alone in a Laundromat, scribbling away in a notebook – another little snapshot to add to his image as a loner.

He pulled his clothes from the dryer about fifteen minutes before closing time. He folded up the jerseys, shorts and other clothes and stuffed them back in his backpack. Seemed silly to fold them before cramming them into a small space, but he made the effort anyway. He made the short ride back to his hotel room and was in bed by a little after nine o'clock. He read for a half hour before turning out the light and rolling on his right side.

Before closing his eyes, he reached over with his right hand to spin his wedding ring three times.

He did it for the first time several years ago when his hands were swollen, and he spun the ring to ease the discomfort. It soon became a mental trigger that it was time to shut off his thoughts and get some sleep. He did it every night, and it worked most of the time.

Most of the time.

XV

Michael slept reasonably well for the second night in a row, something of a record lately.

The bed was nothing special, but of course it was an upgrade from a sleeping bag on the ground. He had decided the night before not to take a day off here in Lincoln City, but he did plan to take a more leisurely morning. He threw on the same clothes he had on last night and walked out the door only half awake.

He hadn't been down to the beach yet, and he thought that needed to be remedied first thing. He stopped by the coffee shop two doors down from the hotel and bought a cup. There was a coffee maker in the room and a pot in the lobby, but hotel coffee had not yet made an upgrade the way that the restaurants had. A poor cup was usually better than no cup, but since the coffee house was only a short distance away he decided to start the day off right.

Black coffee in hand, he crossed the street and headed to the beach. Buildings separated the beach from street through most of the town, but near the state park the view was unobstructed. As soon as he reached the beach, Mike kicked off his flip flops and put skin to sand. There were a few people walking along the beach, but the winds were calm and the skies kite free.

Walking a crooked line toward the surf, he noticed off to his right the place where the lake emptied into the ocean. Calling this a river seemed a bit of a stretch, but he supposed calling it the "world's shortest" gave the town something else to put on their brochure.

When he was riding back home, he often saw folks out walking their dogs along the paths in the early morning, coffee cup in hand. They often looked unshowered, unshaven, half awake – and content. This seemed to be a more enlightened way to start the day, rather than getting in the miles to stave off love handles. Walking along the beach was definitely an upgrade to his typical morning routine, and a bounding dog would only improve the experience.

He reached the surf line, set down his flip flops and walked straight in. The forty-five degree water enveloped his legs and knocked away any cobwebs the caffeine had failed to clear. It wasn't as refreshing as at the end of a long ride in the sunshine, but it still felt pretty good.

As he stood knee deep in the ocean, a thought came to him. Water makes up a majority of our body weight, and it covers most of the Earth's surface as well. This simple combination of hydrogen and oxygen supports life everywhere. It endlessly cycles through plants, animals, soil, oceans, air and back again. The same water that sustained this city's namesake or some unknown shepherd could be coursing through his body right now. And it would move on to bring life to something else in a connection he could hardly comprehend.

It seemed all powerful, right down to the molecular level. Its particular shape and electrical charge creates a strong magnetic pull between the molecules, enough to create a skin on a glass of water. Maybe that is why we are drawn so forcefully to the sea. His body was pulled to rejoin the water in the ocean, while the ocean crashed against his skin trying to get back in.

He stared at the incoming waves for ten minutes until his legs grew numb. It was a peaceful scene, and he imagined the world would be a better place if everyone woke up this way. A quiet moment to gather your thoughts and offer up thanks before you faced the demands of the day, instead of rolling out of bed at a dead run.

He didn't have a time clock to punch this morning, but he did have another eighty miles to get to his next stop. He took a long last breath and turned away from the waves and headed back.

He made use of the shower one more time to rinse off the sand and warm up his muscles. The morning shower and freshly laundered cycling clothes made him feel extra clean, and a little pang of regret that he had to leave the luxury of the hotel behind. Almost as souvenirs, he packed away the soaps and mini shampoo bottles for the campsite showers down the road. A quick stop at the office to check out and drop off the key, and he was on the road before 9:00 am. It was odd that 9 o'clock now felt really late.

The route today was pretty much a straight shot down the coast. Highway 101 stayed within eyesight of the coast for much of the day, passing through a few towns along the way to Florence. Maybe it was his peaceful walk in the ocean to start the day, or the simplicity of today's route, but for whatever reason, he paused frequently to take in the views of the ocean and take a few photos. There were a number of smaller coves and rock islands punctuating the coastline, and every turn seemed to reveal a new angle on the beautiful scene.

At around the twenty mile mark, he took a quieter side road called Otter Crest Loop. It was a one-way road and it seemed expressly built to make a traveler pause and reflect for a short moment. Trees crowded the road with only a thin mossy strip of grass separating them from the pavement, allowing only flickers of light and sound to pass through. Even time seemed to slow somehow. The one mile loop had a designated bike lane, but Michael had the road and the moment to himself.

He stopped for breakfast near Newport, probably the largest town he would see on the route today. He was a couple of hours into his day, and he could use some food to go along with the cup of coffee that had been swimming around his stomach. He stopped at a place that had a red sign that promised pizza, bread, pastries and espresso. The building had the weathered gray, cedar shake siding he saw everywhere in these seaside towns.

He parked his bike against one of the wood planters outside and walked into the small shop. It was still morning, so he wasn't quite ready for pizza. Cold pizza makes for a great breakfast, but for some reason hot pizza doesn't have the same appeal for him early in the day.

One of the promised pastries was a plate-sized cinnamon roll. It was a spiral of thin layers, baked to a perfect caramelized brown. No need for white frosting on this beauty. The accompanying Americano was nearly as large, served in something more like a soup bowl than a coffee cup.

The day was warming up, so he took his breakfast outside to one of the sidewalk tables, and he took time to enjoy the meal. Not that he could have rushed through a cinnamon roll of that size. He was not getting much nutrition these days, living mostly on caffeine and sugar. He was probably down a pound or two with all the riding, but he would definitely need to return to more balanced meals when he got off the road.

But he would worry about that later. He was doing his best to stay in the moment, though it was difficult to keep the past and future entirely at bay. Some people live in the future, some in the past, but the happiest seemed to live most often in the present. Michael definitely lived in the past, focusing on old mistakes instead of relishing the day, or pressing forward to new discoveries. He hoped this trip would do something to interrupt that pattern.

The remainder of the route was much like the morning – endless views of the ocean, a few difficult climbs, and plenty of places to pull off and take a picture. The entire country lay off his left shoulder as he rode alone, clinging to the edge as if he might fall off.

The winds came up in earnest shortly after breakfast. They came steadily from the south so there were fewer side gusts, but he rode into the teeth of the wind for the remainder of the day.

He rode with his hands low in the drops of the handlebars, hunching his body down into a tight ball to get out of the wind, but it didn't seem to make much difference. It felt like one person had a hand against his helmet holding him back, while another clung to the trailer and dug in his heels. As hard as he pressed on the pedals, the only thing that increased was his sense of frustration. He did his best to accept and tune it out, but with only limited success. This wind seemed less random. Today it felt personal.

About ten miles shy of the campground in Florence, he rode by the Sea Lion Caves. He had been there once as a kid and remembered that it had been a pretty cool experience. An elevator descended from the cliffs to caves filled with hundreds of barking sea lions. He remembered it being massive to his young eyes, very deep and several stories tall, and he was tempted to stop to see if the scale was a trick of memory.

Though he had been happy to stop repeatedly today, the wind had beaten him down some and he wasn't up for a tour of the caves this time around. The childhood memory was safe from being disproved for now.

Another memory popped into his head instead. He remembered his first bike.

It was red Schwinn with 20 inch wheels, white handgrips, and a big metal guard that circled the chain so you couldn't catch your pant leg in it. He had that bike for years, eventually pulling off the chain guard, putting on knobby tires, and replacing the chrome handlebars with a flat black, motocross style. He rode that thing until it rusted away, but he could still picture it in its pristine, factory condition.

Most of his friends had bikes before he did, so he had learned to ride by borrowing theirs. When his parents bought him his own bike, he rode off without training wheels or his father running along behind to steady him. He hadn't thought about it before, but he had sort of robbed his Dad of that moment. With another stab of pain, he realized that kind of moment was lost for him as well.

He pulled over at a designated viewpoint just past the caves. He stared out at the incoming waves for a while and tried to wash his mind clean. There were a number of other tourists there, and Mike again offered to take a picture for one of the couples. When they offered to do the same for him, he actually took them up on it this time. This was the first real picture of himself on the trip. He stood behind his bike and trailer to get the full effect.

Though the winds had eased slightly, the ride through Florence was still slow going. Florence was the first town in days that felt like a typical city. There were several one-story strips of stores, and the road was dotted with gas stations and fast-food joints. And there were more traffic signals to go along with the increase in commerce.

He stopped off at a Safeway to stock up on supplies. For road food, he mixed together pretzels, nuts and dried cranberries from the bulk bins. Energy bars do the trick, but after a while he got tired of all the prepackaged sugar. For dinner, he grabbed a deli sandwich and made a salad at the salad bar. With the cinnamon roll still in his stomach and on his mind, he grabbed a couple of bananas as well.

The high winds of the day made him think that the forecast for rain the next day might be accurate, so he bought a box of large garbage bags to try to further rainproof his gear.

The campground was at the outskirts of town, just past the river that seemed to define the southern edge. He rode into JM Honeyman Memorial Park at around four o'clock in the afternoon, and did a quick ride around the grounds before settling on a spot.

He went through his regular routine of setting up camp, and he hadn't lost his touch from the night in the hotel. The surrounding trees did a decent job at blocking out much of the wind, but there was still a steady breeze rippling the tent fabric.

Once his tent was up and his gear was stowed, he went for a walk to stretch out his legs. The park was a couple miles inland from the ocean, but he had spied a lake within the park. He walked down to the water's edge, but resisted the temptation to wade in.

There was a boat launch, and he walked to the end of the accompanying dock and sat down. Sunset wouldn't be for a while, but the sun was starting to lose some of its power to heat the day. But even with the breeze it was still pleasant, and he sat with his legs crossed into a lotus position and stared at the water.

He slowly twisted his torso to the left and then right in an attempt to keep his back loose. His body of invincible youth had been replaced by one with kinks and pains that never went away entirely. He had come to know, and mostly accept, these limitations, but he did what he could to minimize the damage. He stretched before every ride, and he tried to walk for a few minutes afterward, knowing that tomorrow would be better for it.

After a half hour by the water, he strolled back to his campsite and grabbed his clothes and quarters for a shower. There was no sand or saltwater to rinse off, and the battering winds had blown away any sweat before it dampened his clothes, but an evening shower was part of the camping routine. Plus he figured that the warm water on his back might help keep the muscles a little loose. After riding most of the day hunched over in the drops, he wanted to pamper his back as much as possible.

Back at the campsite, he pulled out his sandwich and salad dinner along with his notebook and settled into the nearby picnic table for the next hour or two. The words weren't coming to him this evening, so he pulled out the guitar and strummed his two note song for a while.

He had opted against getting beer at the store this time around, and he missed it a little bit. But he was still struggling with whether he was depending on alcohol. It was naturally a depressant, and he didn't need any help in that respect.

XVI

They were at Alki.

Mike sat in the soft sand just out of reach of the more compacted tide line. It was a beautiful day, and he sat with his heels dug in and his elbows on his knees. A slight breeze tickled at the hair on his arms, threatening to start a wave of goose bumps. He was watching his son run in and out of the waves, playing his own game of chase.

Excitement bubbled up in the boy until it popped in explosive giggles. He tried to catch the waves in his hands, splashing the surface of the water with his tiny hands, drenching his hair until the curls hung limply against his face. His eyes twinkled like the light dancing off the waves. He was beautiful, the embodiment of joy.

Mike heard an awful screech of brakes and the sound of rubber sliding across pavement. The familiar sound stretched out, a tortuous wind up to the sickening sound of twisting metal and breaking glass. Mike was up off the sand and turned toward the road in a moment, in time to see his car plowed into the concrete embankment.

He lunged toward the accident, his feet slipping out from underneath him and pitching him to the sand. In a flash, the sun disappeared, and the sky darkened to a bruised purple. He halted and spun around toward the water. He needed to get his son before tending to the wreckage.

His boy was gone. He was no longer splashing happily in the waves. Mike whipped his head to the left and right, panic rising like bile. The beach was empty.

He looked out into the ocean and saw the boy bobbing in the waves, his laughing silenced. A cold pressure wrapped its arms around Mike, slowing his movements, as everything around him sped up. The wind spun into a frenzy, and the boy disappeared behind the rising waves.

Michael plunged in and swam through the churning water. He would see a flash of pale skin pop out the waves aim for it, only to lose track of it seconds later. When he finally locked onto his son, he was impossibly far away, caught in some other-worldly rip tide. No matter how fast Mike swam, the boy shot farther out of his reach.

Salt stung his eyes and blurred his vision. Water replaced air in his lungs. He could no longer see his son. Everything went black. He sank. He failed.

He woke up.

Air rushed into his lungs, and he looked around in a panic trying to figure out where he was. The phantoms of the nightmare receded; the details of the boy's face washed away. His eyes returned to the present like a camera aperture adjusting to a sudden increase in light, the walls of the tent coming into darker focus.

Insomnia had kept him up to the point where he wasn't sure he would ever sleep again. His mind raced through the evening, bouncing from painful image to non sequitur thought. There were many nights when he couldn't get his brain to stop chattering. Getting things down on paper sometimes helped him clear things out, but what little he wrote last night only stirred the pot.

After a few impotent hours, he gave up trying and went for a walk in the darkness. Sleep was a shifting phantom. If you focused on it, it would disappear. You had to look at it out of the corner of your eye like an eclipse, or let it sneak up on you like the advice about love – you can only find it when you aren't looking.

Last night he stopped trying to keep the thoughts at bay and let them push and elbow their way through his brain as he walked. When the din subsided, he went back to lie down. It felt like his mind had cleared only to twist into turmoil as soon as his head hit the pillow again.

Although he had read that alcohol interrupts your sleep pattern, a drink or two generally helped him cross the plane into sleep. He wished he had something to drink. For a moment he considered pedaling into town, but he didn't know if you could buy booze in the middle of the night here in Oregon.

After vainly trying to shut off his mind through force of will, he turned on his headlamp to read. He read for hours and through many pages, but must have fallen asleep at some point. In the morning he woke with the book bent underneath him, the headlamp still strapped to his head, the battery now dead.

He felt battered and disoriented from the nightmare. The hard ground had its effect as well, and he woke up stiff and sore. When he was able to straighten up, his lower back and glutes rebelled. He was definitely in better shape, but it was hard to tell by the way he felt each morning. His morning body was angry at the foolish athletic indulgence of the day before, like a pounding head raging at the alcoholic after a hard night.

~

He had two more days of riding in Oregon. Today's route would take him seventy miles south to Bandon, and it was another eighty-five miles to Brookings near the California border. He had been on the road for a while now, and the next couple of days kind of blended together in his mind.

The few things that stuck out in his mind from the ride to Bandon were a lighthouse, a bridge, a set of hills and a couple of dogs. And of course, the rain.

His morning route went by a lighthouse south of Reedsport that marked the opening to the Umpqua River. According to the sign, the original lighthouse was built in 1857, and was the first in the Oregon territory. It was destroyed by a flood a few years later, but rebuilt in 1891. Lighthouses were certainly critical to early navigation, but Mike wondered if they were anything more than historical markers these days.

The open view from the lighthouse did give him an unobstructed view of the gray-black rain clouds almost upon him. Not long after reading the plaque about the 19th century floods, the first real rain of the trip started falling. Soon the gentle rain so common in the Pacific Northwest was ratcheted up to a sky opening deluge more typical of tropical storms of the south.

Mike quickly dug out his rain jacket and was thankful he had taken the time to wrap all his gear in an extra garbage bag layer the night before. The trailer was filed with a mass of black plastic, accented with some gray duct tape holding two bags together around the guitar.

The first rain after a long dry period will loosen all the oil dripped from cars and wash it to the side of the road. The oil made the wet surface that much more slick, particularly the painted white lines at the edge of the road. The winds were nowhere near as strong as the day before, but they still pushed the rain sideways of vertical.

The raindrops were large enough that they struck his rain jacket with hail-like force. The water crashing to the ground drowned out the sound of everything but car tires plowing through the slick of water. It quickly grew to that point of ridiculousness that a sane person would have long left. He pedaled with his head down through a wall of water and sound, trying his best to laugh at the absurdity.

The remembered bridge was the Coos Bay Bridge into the town of North Bend. He could see the bridge in profile as the road approached it, and it was an odd mix of bounding concrete arches at either end, with a bow tie shaped span of cantilevered steel in the middle. A sign near the entrance of the bridge noted that when the bridge was built, it was the longest in Oregon. Every town seemed to have its own claim to fame, however small.

Unfortunately, the sign also noted that it was illegal for bicyclists to hold up traffic. Bicyclists were restricted to the narrow sidewalk where they were instructed to walk, rather than ride their bikes. The sidewalk was more like a narrow ledge not much wider than the trailer, so Mike felt no temptation to disobey the sign and ride across. The bridge was a mile long, but seemed much longer pushing a bike through the rain.

Not long after crossing the bridge into North Bend, the recommended route left Highway 101 and headed west through town. Mike decided to stop for lunch and to get out of the rain for a while before continuing on.

He picked the first fast food joint he came across and parked his bike under the eaves. People were staring at him through the restaurant windows, probably remarking at what an idiot he was to be out riding in the rain. He squeezed his hands into a fist and wrung the water out of his gloves giving them more ammunition.

He headed straight for the bathroom and peeled off his outer layer of clothing. He shook out his jacket before thinking what a mess he was going to make on their tile floors. There was already a yellow, "wet floor" pylon by the door, so clearly people had already been dragging the rain in. He rinsed his hands under warm water to break through the chill, and there was a painful tingle as they thawed out.

Since they were already soaked, he decided to rinse out his gloves in hot water to at least warm them up. He spent several minutes with his hands and head under the hot air dryer, occasionally stepping aside so another person could dry his hands. It was a little pointless since it was still raining, but it felt good to dry out if only for a moment.

After eating his burger and fries, he decided to hang out a little longer. The rain had eased off to more of a steady drizzle, and he hoped that he could wait it out. He ordered a cup of coffee, wrapped both hands around the cup and stuck his face over the steaming brew. It really wasn't all that cold outside, but he was soaked to the bone, and the wind had carried away his body heat. After another half an hour, the rain had eased only slightly and he could not justify waiting any longer. He put his still-wet rain gear back on, sending quick shivers through his body.

He rejoined the road heading west, and after about a mile the route turned south to parallel the inlet until it left the city. At that point it became Seven Devils Road, which didn't sound terribly encouraging. Almost immediately the road climbed sharply, and Mike continued to downshift until he found a gear that would allow him to turn the pedals over.

After the initial steep climb, Seven Devils Road became a series of short but steep climbs and descents. He lost track of the number of peaks and valleys, but he was sure there were more than seven that the name of the road seemed to imply. The rain eased as he climbed, and eventually ceased altogether. Soon a steam-like mist rose from the road, and he imagined there was a plume coming off his rain jacket as well.

After a longer and particularly steep climb, the road finally leveled out for good. Not long after cresting the hill and getting his breath and his heart rate down, Mike saw a dog standing in the middle of the road a few blocks away.

Mike instinctively slowed down a bit as he rode toward the dog. The dog stood completely still until Mike rode within a hundred feet of him, and then turned and ran off down the road. After running for about thirty seconds, the dog turned around and stood in the middle of the road, staring back at Mike once again.

Once Mike came within a certain distance, the dog was off once more. This little game went on for a couple more rounds before the dog disappeared around a corner. It was a strange and somehow unsettling encounter. Not long after losing the dog, Mike spied a different dog loose in a yard on the right side of the road up ahead.

He had encountered several dogs while out on past rides, but had not had any major run-ins. He had grown up in a house that always had a dog or two, so he did not have any sort of natural fear when a stray dog approached.

Dogs were typically very protective of their people and property, and would bark to warn off anyone approaching, but there was rarely any lingering menace behind the barking. In his experience, the adage of, "his bark is worse than his bite," was almost always true. If a dog gave chase at all, it was usually half-hearted.

As he approached the dog, he recognized it as a Pit Bull. Pit Bulls had a bad reputation these days. There had been several mauling incidents in the news, and people had even called for banning the breed in some cities.

Mike felt that although the breed might be more troublesome, it was almost always the owner that was the problem. Too many dog owners trained their dogs to be aggressive for their own psychological reasons. As he got a little closer, he noticed that the dog had a chewed length of rope dangling from his collar. Not a good sign.

The dog charged down the gravel driveway, past the incomplete chain link fence and into the road. There were no cars in either direction, so Mike moved left to the opposite side of the road. The dog did not stop at the end of the driveway and kept charging toward the bike. He entered the road just as Mike passed by and gave chase.

He had read several recommendations on what to do when a dog charges including: squirting them with your water bottle, using your tire pump as a weapon, talking nicely or yelling, kicking, and even stopping to take away the fun of the chase. If you stop, for whatever reason, keep the bike between you and the dog. This dog looked like it was interested in more than just the chase.

Mike was pretty tapped out after all the climbing, and with the additional weight of the trailer he could not out-sprint the dog. He used his deepest most authoritative voice to growl, "No!" and, "Go Home!" but the dog just kept coming. The dog seemed to easily match Mike's pace, hovering within a lunge of chomping down on his legs.

He did not want to take his hands off the handlebars to reach for a water bottle or pump, and he figured if he tried to kick it would only piss the dog off. It would take a direct hit to discourage this dog, and once the foot was off the pedal, he would lose any chance to maintain his speed.

Mike stood up out of the saddle so he would have more leverage to throw into the pedal stroke. He touched the brakes to briefly slow down, let the dog shoot pass just a bit, and then hammered the pedals to try to put some distance between him and his pursuer.

It did not work.

Mike just did not have the speed to out run the dog. He tried turning into the dog's path to surprise the dog into slowing, and was soon zigzagging like someone was shooting at him from behind. He was out of energy and options, and was ready to just coast to a stop and see what happened.

Eventually, the dog gave up out of either fatigue or waning interest. The dog peeled off and stood in the middle of the road and kept barking. Maybe Mike had reached some invisible line that the dog considered the protection perimeter. Mike continued on down the road, willing to take luck over skill in dropping the dog.

His legs shook from the effort, and the rest of his body shivered from what might have happened, so once he was out of range of the dog, he lazily turned the pedals without putting much pressure on them. He was basically coasting but kept his legs turning to help pump the blood out of his lower extremities. As he coasted, he wondered (only semi-seriously) if the dogs were working together, and the first dog he saw was some sort of scout.

~

His last full day in Oregon was much less eventful, and much more scenic. Highway 101 hugged the coastline for much of the day, and after a morning fog, the weather was perfect. His tunnel vision seemed to have been washed away with the rain, and it felt like he was stopping every few miles to appreciate another spectacular view of the ocean.

He stopped in Gold Beach for a sit-down lunch of fish and chips, and walked along the waterfront for a bit afterward. The restaurant fronted a small marina, and there were some sea lions stretched out on the water breaks, basking in the afternoon sun. Mike wasn't nearly as sedentary, but he felt like he was mimicking their lazy approach to the day.

He arrived in Brookings to find a campground buzzing with activity. It was surprising after rolling up to so many quiet resting spots, and it took him a while to realize that it was a Friday night. Without work, e-mail or even a daily paper, he had lost track of what day it was. And this particular lapse in memory actually felt good.

He didn't bother to ride through the whole campsite and just took the first open spot he found. The campground sat on a bluff over the ocean, and there was a path down to the beach. He didn't even bother setting up his tent before walking down to stick his legs in the ocean.

His priorities were shifting, and he was less concerned with sticking to a routine and making sure his chores were done. The cold water once again felt good on his legs, but he had found that they were a bit less weary at the end of the ride these days. His fitness must be improving, even if his back made him feel his age each morning.

When he walked back, he noticed that there was actually a little Laundromat in the campground. It was a nice touch and was probably an indication that campers often stayed for more than a long weekend. But he didn't make use of the extra amenities, and just did his normal routine of washing out his riding gear in the sink.

It was a quiet evening, and after eating his convenience store dinner, he turned in early and read himself to sleep. He was a long way from home, but still had a lot of road ahead. Tomorrow he would be crossing into California.

XVII

He was in California – land of sunshine and fake tans, gold rushes and earthquakes, Hollywood governors and enormous statues of Paul Bunyan. His mind had been drifting for what seemed like hours, remembering the week-long journey that had brought him to the California border past the Trees of Mystery. He was finally brought out of his reverie by the sight of a golden bear.

Two golden bears actually. They flanked the entrance to a bridge over the Klamath River. They stood on concrete pedestals and looked away from the bridge, off into the woods where they would rather be. The California state flag had a bear on it, so this seemed to be one more official welcome to the state.

He was some distance inland, but could tell he was somewhere near sea level again. The river was lazy and wide at this point and looked like it had only had a couple of turns remaining before it emptied into the ocean. Mike was feeling a little drowsy himself after resting in motion for several miles, but he suspected that would not last very long. The road was level for now, but he saw more hills to the south.

He set his pedals in motion and felt the weight of the trailer once more. In the thick of a climb, he almost forgot it was there, and it was only when he had to get moving again that he felt the drag of all he was towing behind.

He settled into a comfortable pace, just enough to get the blood pumping through his legs as he knocked the cobwebs out of his head. His mind had been elsewhere, and he only had vague images of the last few miles. He tried once again to bring his focus back to the here and now.

He had looked over the route plan during lunch, and he noticed that the route would leave the highway shortly after crossing the bridge. He could continue along the highway and get where he was going, but it looked like Gerry and his group had taken a side road through the forest. Highway 101 was also called the "Redwood Highway" at this point, but the side road had "scenic parkway" in its title. It sounded like an improvement on something that was already pretty spectacular.

The turnoff came just after he entered Prairie Creek Redwoods State Park, and he was soon enveloped by trees again. The air cooled and thickened, and he could feel the water in the air coat his throat. The road climbed for the next five miles, but it was gradual enough that his head was not slumped over for the effort. Instead of flicking his gaze from the pavement to the horizon as he did during difficult climbs, his head was held high and his focus was above the horizon and into the trees.

The forest drew in and crowded the road. It appeared that when the path had been cleared to put in this road, they took out only what was necessary. Typically, a wider swath was cut so that the only trees near the road were smaller saplings that had grown back after construction. Here there were massive trees, likely hundreds of years old, just off the pavement's edge. Although the road was paved, it felt more like a trail through the woods.

Washington had its own mountains and dense forests, but he had not done nearly enough riding outside of the city. Much of the Olympic Peninsula was classified as a rain forest, and he had been through it by car, but not since he was a kid. He needed to ride through the forest in his own backyard when he returned. One more thing to add to the need-to-do-before-you-die list.

He wanted to keep his bucket list short, though. You have no idea how much time you have left, and saying that you need to do something before you die, places it squarely in the *someday* category when it should be in the *this needs to happen soon* category. He had enough trouble with procrastinating that he didn't need to add a formal list of things he wasn't getting to. But he was halfway to completing his promised trip down the coast, and that was something.

The scenic byway was deserted except for his solitary bicycle. The only man-made sounds were the spinning gears and the tire rubber contacting and releasing from the pavement. The moment felt meditative, and the forest was his own private sanctuary for almost twelve miles. The slope of the downhill was slight, allowing him to maintain forward motion without increasing his speed. He coasted with his eyes in the trees and a stupid grin on his face.

Too late it came to him that he had not picked up anything for dinner. There were no convenience stores in the middle of the forest, so he would be subsisting on energy bars for the evening. Maybe he should have taken up the dessert offer back at the Trees of Mystery.

When the scenic parkway rejoined the highway, it was only fifteen miles and a couple of climbs to make it to the campground. Back out on the highway, his pace picked up again and he was riding into Patrick Point State Park within an hour.

The entrance road was winding and he spent some time checking out the various campsites. In sharp contrast to the Brookings site the night before, this campground was pretty deserted for a Saturday. It was surprising, but maybe there were other attractions a short distance down the road that were more tempting. Or maybe camping just wasn't as popular in California.

Since he had the pick of the place, he pulled into one of the larger group sites at the west end of the campground. It was closer to the ocean overlook, and the showers and bathrooms were steps away. The site was a large circle, similar to a neighborhood cul-de-sac, and he put up his tent near the entrance to the loop. If a large group did come halfway through the weekend and wanted to use it, he probably wouldn't even need to move his tent. He would just be that strange neighbor at the end of the street.

He unloaded his gear and set about putting up his tent. The site was well shaded, and the ground was still a little damp from the rains on Thursday. September was often a great month in Washington, but it was still surprising how little rain there had been. Hopefully, California's sunny reputation would keep the rainy days to one.

The site had a couple of picnic tables and a fire pit in the center of the circle. The fire pit was a stone and mortar thing with a metal grate on top that had gone to rust. One side of the stone circle had given way at some point, so there was an opening for wind to rush in and stoke the fire, or frustrate efforts to get one started.

He hadn't seen a place to purchase firewood at the campsite, but the last campers had left a few pieces of split wood that they didn't get around to burning. Mike decided to hold off on a fire until late in the evening, reasoning it wouldn't take more than an hour or two to burn through the small stack.

Toward the back of the site, he saw a container attached to a tree about five feet off the ground. The box was cabinet sized and had a lockable thumb latch. A small placard said it was a bear box. Mike had never camped in a place that had bear boxes, but he had heard enough stories to understand what they were.

Campers were encouraged (probably required) to put all their food in these boxes to keep it away from the bears. If a bear smelled food in your tent, the thin layer of material between you and the bear was no deterrent. He had heard stories of bears pulling people out of their tents for as little as a candy bar.

Beyond the western edge of the camp site, the land fell away and dropped a few hundred feet down to the ocean. There was a nice filtered view of the horizon through the trees. He saw what he assumed was a path down the hillside to the beach, but he decided to skip his feet-in-the-ocean routine for today.

He headed back to his tent for his toiletry kit, clothes, and roll of quarters so he could shower off. He also grabbed his phone charger so he could top off his phone battery. He hadn't been using it much, but he didn't want to pass up an open plug, especially when he didn't need to worry about another camper walking off with it.

After a quick shower broken up into two coin-operated time periods, he dried off with the camp towel he had brought along. It was one of those quick drying materials and was more a chamois than a towel. It reminded him of those miracle cloths that he saw at every fair these days, but without a similar ability to soak up the cups of water shown in the demonstrations. As he toweled off it felt like the water was being removed by friction and gravity more than anything else. Those hotel towels, roughed from years of use and bleach were looking pretty good right now.

He washed out his cycling clothes in the sink and squeezed them dry as best he could. They were, of course, made with their own sort of miracle fabric so they didn't take as long to dry out either. He brushed his teeth not because he was done eating for the night, but just because he was in the bathroom and was thinking about it. It was probably a good thing he wasn't talking to too many people along the way. His hygiene routine was pretty sketchy these days.

He would normally drape his clothes over the bent poles of the tent to dry, but there was only filtered sunshine hitting his campsite. He went over to one of the picnic tables to drag it out of the shade. The table top was carved with initials, and there were several stickers plastered to the metal legs including a weathered "Shit Happens" bumper sticker. He put the table into the middle of the cul-de-sac to grab as much sunshine as he could and flattened out his damp clothes and towel to dry. He brought out his backpack of distractions and sat at the table to read in the sun.

He stayed on the bench, reading and writing until the sun passed completely below the tree line on its way to the horizon. The air cooled, but he didn't want to start the fire just yet. He went back to the tent, put on a sweatshirt and gathered up his food to put into the bear box, stuffing a bar and the bag of trail mix in his pocket for dinner later.

After securing his provisions against predators, he disconnected his bike from the trailer and flipped it upside-down on the picnic table. He spent a half an hour checking for anything that looked out of place, tightening up any screws or bolts that may have worked their way loose, and then cleaned and re-lubed the chain. The tires seemed to be in good shape, with no noticeable cuts or gouges. He turned the wheels and touched his hands lightly to the spinning rubber, feeling for an unseen bit of glass that could work its way in over time.

He took a break and went to the restroom, and as he returned, he looked at his upside-down bike sitting on the picnic table.

When out on a group ride, it is common to see other cyclists at the side of the road. Many are just taking a break, but others are trying to fix something that has gone wrong - a flat tire, a dropped chain, or just trying to locate a ticking noise that won't go away. An upside-down bicycle is a sure sign something is wrong. On larger rides with many riders, it won't be a minute before you hear, "Are you doing okay? Do you have everything you need?"

When you offer help to a bicyclist on the side of the road, ninety-nine times out of a hundred they will smile and wave you on. But some at the side of the road may not know exactly what to do, or have the right tools to make the repair. Even experienced riders may need a hand if they have already run across several problems and are out of supplies or patience. He had seen more than one bicycle thrown down in disgust.

Michael had read long ago that once we accept that life will be challenging, we transcend it. The fact that life is difficult no longer matters – it is just part of the deal and there is little you can do to change it. You can only change the way you look at the difficulties.

To complain about all the little things that go wrong in your day-to-day life implies that it is somehow unexpected. That everything should just fall into place, that life itself should be easy. To shout at the rain would seem about as sane and effective. But sometimes the tiniest of straws are the final ones.

Mike knew he had a very fortunate life. He had his health, a loving family and friends. He lived in a society where he did not need to worry about clean water or the availability of food, and he tried to keep the minor annoyances in perspective. His life had been largely untouched by tragedy, but now he was unhinged and flailing, all those lessons of perspective forgotten.

Now it was Michael broken down, and he didn't have the tools to fix what was wrong. He hadn't reached out for help, and there was no one to see his upside-down bike. Even if someone stopped to ask if he needed help, would he wave them on with an "I'm fine," not wanting to complain or put a dent in his shield of self-reliance?

The shadows grew longer as he worked on the bike, and by the time he was done, he needed his headlamp to illuminate some of the smaller parts. Satisfied that the bike was road-worthy for another day, he tethered it to the trailer again. He grabbed the coffee pot and filled it up from the water tap outside the bathroom. It was time for fire.

When he bought things at the store, he opted for paper over plastic and hung onto the bags as fire starters. He was no Boy Scout, but he had camped often enough to be prepared. There were still plenty of empty pages left in his notebook, and he had dipped into those when necessary, but he preferred to fill them with words before burning.

He walked around the perimeter of the campsite to look for dead twigs to help get the fire going. He found some dried lichen on the forest floor, and he made use of that as well. It made him feel slightly more resourceful than using notebook paper.

The wind was down and the combination of paper, lichen and twigs caught rather easily. The last set of campers had left three quarter-rounds of firewood, so it would not be a large or long lasting fire, but it would do fine for coffee and some brief ambiance. He put the percolator on the grill and waited for the water to boil. The grill was kind of high for the size of fire he was able to build, so it would be a while for the coffee to brew. The sun was almost at the horizon, and he wandered toward the edge of the hill to watch it go down.

When he came back to the fire, the water was boiling and the decaf percolating. He picked up the pot and with his headlamp pointed at the spout, poured a little coffee on the ground to see how dark it was. It looked close enough for camp coffee, so he filled up his travel mug. He sat down on the picnic bench and pulled out an energy bar to go with the coffee. He liked his coffee hot, but the camp coffee was just off the boil, so he stared into the fire as he let it cool.

His eyes were focused on the flames, but his mind was elsewhere. Memories, faces and random images flickered behind his eyes, but tonight they were semi-transparent and he could look through them without feeling their full impact. He was lost in his thoughts for some time, and he didn't even remember eating his nutrition bar dinner or drinking his coffee. He could not seem to stop the painful images from flashing through his mind, but his mind seemed to have adapted a certain line of defense.

He had no idea what time it was. He had not been wearing a watch, and his only time keeper was his bike computer or the location of the sun in the sky. Time was kind of irrelevant on a trip like this, so he was usually happy to remain clueless. However late it was, he was ready to call it a night. He spread the coals around the fire pit to let the fire die down. He threw his stuff back in the tent and trailer, washed out the percolator and refilled it to douse the fire.

The cool water over the hot coals made a satisfying sizzling noise and sent a plume of steam and ash into the air. After the air cleared, the remaining coals looked like a series of glowing eyes staring back at him from the darkness. After brushing his teeth, he poured another pot-full on the fire and that took care of all but the smallest embers.

Back in his tent, he read his thriller novel for about an hour until eyes grew heavy. He switched off his headlamp, tossed it in a corner and rolled over on to his right side to go to sleep. He felt a lump in his right pocket and realized that he still had the bag of trail mix on him.

Instantly paranoid, he fumbled around in the darkness to find his light. Breathing a little heavily, he unzipped the tent and dashed across the campsite to put the food into the bear box. He had entertained thoughts about ending it all not that long ago, but a bear mauling was not what he had in mind.

As he passed the fire on the way to his tent, there was a single ember staring back at him.

XVIII

Mike awoke gasping for breath.

Peaceful sleep was elusive once more, and his mind continued to cheat his body of rest. The most frustrating part was that even after eight or nine hours of sleep, he still woke exhausted like he had been working through the night. He definitely felt worse after a five hour night, but he never woke up refreshed. But his night wasn't interrupted by a bear encounter, so he had that going for him.

Out of bed, dress, brush teeth, put on sunscreen, fill water bottles, roll up sleeping bag then tent, pack the trailer, go. Even running on fumes, he was becoming more efficient first thing in the morning.

He rolled out of camp and found an early rhythm. The road had just enough bumps and dips to forestall any monotony that might send him drifting back to sleep. At mile ten there was a pretty sharp downhill that brought him out of the forest and back down to sea level. He passed through a few towns early on, but he waited until Eureka at mile twenty-five to stop for breakfast. It would be the largest town for the day, so he figured he'd make a long stop and swing by a grocery store as well.

Eureka is on an interior bay, and Highway 101 hugged the edge of the water on the way into town. He had been settling for a cup of coffee and a pastry the last few days, and after having an energy bar for dinner the night before, he was ready for full breakfast. Coffee and bacon made life worth living, or at least made getting out of bed a little easier.

He found a diner and took a seat at the counter. He loved to find restaurants that had counters near the kitchen. If the place was busy, he wouldn't be taking up a booth that could seat four people, and sitting at the counter satisfied some aesthetic need. It made him feel like a regular wherever he was, and he was within easy reach of the coffee pot.

It was actually kind of quiet at the diner this morning, so he had barely picked out a stool before the waitress had a menu and a cup of coffee in front of him. The breakfast choices were limited to the staples, with no exotic omelet combinations or odd fruits showing up on waffles. Broccoli may be a fine vegetable, but he didn't think it belonged in an omelet.

Mike normally craved something sweet, but after living on energy bars and coffee-stand muffins, he opted for a Denver Omelet instead. It came with toast and home potatoes, and he added a side of bacon to keep the universe in alignment.

Bacon was actually the darling product these days, showing up in recipes for nearly everything, and as flavorings for coffee, vodka, mayonnaise and even air fresheners. Mike loved bacon, but was happy to keep it where it belonged, sitting next to eggs and on the occasional sandwich or burger.

He sat facing the kitchen pass-through window and could see the tickets hanging in front of the cook. Mike enjoyed watching a short-order cook in action, juggling multiple orders and cooking stations, timing everything so that they all hit the plate freshly steaming. It is a thing of beauty to watch someone who is good at his job, and the cook in front of him this morning looked to be a virtuoso in his particular art form. He was not slammed with orders, but the fluidity of his motions and steady gaze made him look unflappable.

His breakfast was up at the pass-through and the cook pinged his metal spatula against the grill three times as a signal to the waitress that food was ready to be picked up. The omelet was in front of Mike seconds later, and the waitress was back in three minutes to check on things and top off his coffee. If only everything worked so efficiently.

The food was good, not spectacular, and exactly what he expected. Mike borrowed the sports page from the other guy at the counter and read through scores and game recaps that he didn't much care about, but enjoyed reading this morning just the same.

He enjoyed watching football and baseball, but did not get wrapped up in all the statistics and minutiae. He could not quote batting averages, and would be hard pressed to remember who won the Super Bowl the year before.

He didn't understand the appeal of Fantasy Football or the time people devoted to managing their teams. He would much rather enjoy a single game on TV than to spend the afternoon tracking how "his" quarterback and receiver were connecting, even though they were playing on different teams. It seemed like an unnecessary complication of leisure activity, but to each his own.

He did admire the passion people put into it, though, even if he couldn't understand their choice of focus. Mike was in no position to judge since he couldn't point to any one thing that he threw all his energies behind. He lacked a passionate pursuit, and it left him feeling like he was drifting down a river without a rudder.

No, he did not understand the obsession with Fantasy Football, comic books, trading cards, or anything that inspired conventions, but he did envy the people who found and pursued their passion.

After cleaning his plate and finishing his third cup of coffee, he was ready to move on. He left money for the bill and tip on the counter, and waved to the waitress on the way out. She had told him where to find a grocery store as well as an ATM so he could restock his dwindling cash reserves.

He stopped by the grocery store first and picked up dinner for the night. He tried to find something of more substance than energy bars but that didn't need to be refrigerated since the cool of evening was a long way off. He settled on some noodle and potato dishes that could be reconstituted with a little boiling water, along with some fruit and beef jerky. Still not a very well rounded meal, but it was an upgrade from an energy bar. He remembered he could just get cash back when he paid for his groceries, so he could skip the stop at the bank. He took a roll of quarters as part of his change.

It was sort of weird to be carrying cash again. When debit credit cards came out, he initially used them for his gas and grocery stops, but felt silly paying for a five dollar meal with plastic, even if it did come right out of his checking account. But it was a slippery slope, and eventually he was whipping out the card for a single cup of coffee. For a variety of reasons, he wanted to primarily use cash on this trip. Within a week, he noticed that he paid more attention to the money going out when it wasn't disguised in plastic.

The sun was still short of the highest point in the sky, but with no clouds holding it back, it was already getting warm. The sun felt nice on his back, and breakfast felt good in his belly. He mounted his bike and headed back toward the highway.

The highway paralleled the bay for another five miles, but he couldn't see the open ocean. The bay is protected by two thin strips of land, extended like arms clutching the bay to the mainland. He eventually saw a narrow opening between the breakwaters with a defined channel for the boats to enter into the protected bay. At the tip of the right arm was a municipal airport, so this city seemed to be built to be a portal to all types of traffic.

The highway turned inland at the south end of the bay, and after a few more miles he was climbing another bloody hill. With a full belly and plenty of daylight left, Mike did not try to beat the hill into submission. He rode slowly to digest the food and scenery.

Being on a bike afforded him a much better view of the land versus speeding by in a car, but he still found himself zoning out and missing the details. Biking, and this trip specifically should be his passion right now. Regardless of the motivation, this trip was an amazing opportunity, and he should embrace each day with the passion that others spend on their hobbies.

The sun was still too high in the sky to be filtered by the increasing trees, but he felt a dip in the temperature and a slight change in the moisture in the air. Riding along the ocean there was always a level of humidity, but back in the forests there was a different type of moisture in the air rising up from the ground sheltered by forest. Trying to explain how one moisture is different from another sounded crazy in his head, but it was a distinction he felt nonetheless.

There was a fair amount of traffic competing for space on the road, but the shoulders were adequate to avoid much confrontation. The width of the pavement to the right of the white fog line seemed to define how much focus he had to put into where he was riding. As the path narrowed, he had less brain space to devote to the beauty passing by. Here, the shoulder space was wide enough to balance out the frequency of cars passing by, allowing him to take a look around once in a while.

As the road traveled inland, it paralleled a river headed in the opposite direction. The road traveled a slightly straighter path, and the river would cross back and forth underneath the road every couple of miles. There were no scenic overlooks to pull out on that screamed, "Hey, look at me!" The forest was one large canvas that needed to be taken in as a whole rather than picked apart to find the one defining feature. He did his best to store mental pictures rather than reach for the camera.

The route left Highway 101 for a smaller side road at around mile sixty. He believed that it was the original road through this area and that the highway had been straightened out at this point to speed up the traffic that was just passing through.

Gerry had mentioned this stretch of road specifically when he told the tale of his trip, so Mike made sure to highlight this diversion on his map. He took the exit ramp and then turned left to pass under the highway. He then made an immediate right and was stopped short by what he saw.

He was now on the Avenue of the Giants, and for once there was no exaggeration in the name.

He had been through so many roadside attractions that claimed to be the *biggest* this or the *largest* that. He had seen the "largest, free-standing cuckoo clock" in his travels many years ago, and like many other attractions with such grand claims, he walked away thinking, "Meh, I thought it would be bigger." But the Avenue of the Giants lived up to its lofty name.

He pulled over to the side of the road near a sign welcoming him to the Humboldt Redwoods State Park. The sign's lettering appeared to have been routered out free-hand before being painted yellow to stand out against the wood canvas. Below the larger welcome sign was a map of the Avenue, along with some historical and touristy information.

According to the sign, the Avenue of the Giants was a thirty-two mile long road traveling through the largest redwood park in all of California. The 53,000 acre forest was home to the world's tallest trees, growing to heights of over 360 feet, and living as long as 2,000 years.

As the sign said, "the trees represent a 'living museum' of what was once the greatest forest on earth." A bold claim, but one Mike could not begin to dispute as he stood underneath these giants of the forest.

He had leaned his bike up against one of these enormous trees, and the length of his bike and trailer combo made it less than halfway around the tree's circumference. These trees were incredible, and he was amazed to see how small his bike looked by comparison.

He walked back out to the road and looked down its length to the south. The large trees crowded the road, and their branches bent over the road to make it look like you were literally tunneling through the forest. A friend of Mike's called this canopy effect of the trees a "hover", and this was certainly the best example he had ever seen.

There are things of beauty that are said to take your breath away, and Mike could feel it happening here. He found himself unconsciously holding his breath, overwhelmed by the magnitude of the trees. Their size, age, and sheer number, and the feeling that some fabled creature might step out of the story books and walk up to him.

His chest unclenched and he began taking in deep, cleansing breaths as his mind tried to take in the scene. He was extremely thankful that these sorts of places have been saved from the developer's bulldozer, and have been preserved for the renewal of generations.

He took several photos of the entrance and the tunnel of trees, knowing already that they would not translate. He would do his best to describe the moment to others, and he knew the photos would only give a glimpse of what it was like to actually be here. But the photos would at least provide him with a launching point for his memory, and he hoped that he would be able to describe it well enough to get people to see it for themselves.

He both wished someone was there with him, and was happy he was alone. Alone, he could stand in one place taking in the scene, without interruption or concern that he would look silly. He did not have to concern himself whether the other person was bored or not, and could linger to his heart's content.

At the same time, he wished he had his wife or someone else special to share the moment with. A moment or memory shared seems to magnify in significance by more than a simple factor of two.

After a few lazy 360 degree turns to look at the forest around him, he decided he had captured as much as he was going to. Not a single car had passed in the time he had been stopped, adding to the feeling that he had just stepped into another world entirely.

He walked back to his bike and rode through the dirt turnout and back to the paved surface. As he rode through the beautiful hover, he could tell he had a glassy, star-struck look in his eyes and a dopey smile on his face. And it was wonderful.

The sun wouldn't normally be low enough in the sky at this point to be blocked out, but the trees were so tall and densely packed that he rode through more shade than sunlight. He rode very slowly through the seemingly endless forest, thankful for so many things, not the least of which was the continuing absence of cars. Since the road was his alone for now, he rode right down the middle, subconsciously following the double line like it was the yellow brick road.

The scale of the trees was hard to take in. The sight of his bike up against the tree trunk had given him some perspective, but his eyes began to swim as the massive pillars went by like fence posts. Then he saw something off to the right side of the road that made his eyes go wide. Through the trees he saw something that looked like an explosion somehow petrified in wood. He pulled over to a stop, and walked through the trees to get a better look.

What he had seen from the road was the immense root ball of a redwood giant lying prone on the forest floor. All of the soil had been washed away, and at the center of the root system was an empty space that went several feet up the tree trunk. From that hollow center, roots shot out in all directions like shrapnel tracers frozen in flight.

As he got closer he could see the gnarled twists and turns the root paths took, but the picture of how they radiated out from that center remained. They shot out from all degrees of that center circle, but the outer perimeter of their reach did not form a perfect circle of their own. It was more oval shaped, and how the tree had come to rest it was wider than it was tall.

He walked around to look at the tree it had once supported, and the trunk of the massive tree was fluted like a Roman column. It is easy to forget how much the architecture of our man-made creations is based on the natural world.

He walked back around to the root ball and took out his camera. He took a few photos, but knew he needed to get something else in the picture to provide perspective as to how large this thing really was. His bike was back out on the road, and it would be difficult to walk it through the dense forest to set it next to the tree. He decided to try out the timer on his camera for the first time.

It took him a few minutes to search through the menus to find the setting, and then some trial and error to find a level spot where it would stay still, but he found a relatively flat rock about thirty feet from the tree. He clicked the shutter and dashed back to the tree in time to see the flashing indicator rapid fire before the picture was taken. The first shot was a little off-center, but the second try produced a good shot.

Now that he had the perspective of his five foot seven inch frame, it looked like the root ball was about fifteen feet high and twenty-five feet across. Before walking back out to the road, he snapped a couple of pictures of the tree in profile but could not get it all in. He had no clue how tall the tree was because the top extended too far into the forest to see. He laughed to himself that he "could not see the tree for the forest."

He was back out on the road for only a short while when he passed by a designated roadside attraction. Even with incredible scenery in every direction, the National Forest was not immune to trying to grab tourists' attention, though this one seemed pretty subdued by comparison. He rode through the tiny parking lot to find the "Immortal Tree."

According to the sign, the tree was between 950 to 1000 years old with a trunk diameter of fourteen and a half feet. It said the original height was 298 feet, but that the current height was only 248 feet. The tree had survived the lightning that removed its top, the logger's axe, a forest fire in 1908, and a flood in 1964. Though there were no branches within thirty feet of the ground, a line at the bottom of the sign asked tourists to "please not climb the tree."

The carved sign he read at the entrance to the forest said that the trees could live to two thousand years, but for some reason he didn't think about the length of time until he saw this one-thousand year old specimen. With our human life span of something around seventy-five years, it is hard to wrap your head around all that has gone on in the thousand years this tree has been alive.

Our own country was a paltry 230 years old, and when this tree was just a sapling, paper was only then arriving in Europe. It is odd how millions of years are easy to accept when talking about dinosaurs, but a thousand years can cause complete brain lock up when staring at a tree.

Another mile or two down the road, he passed a sign that told him he was only 239 miles from San Francisco. It felt weird to put an *only* in front of 239 miles, especially on a bike, but his sense of distance had changed over the past couple of weeks. Of course, the bustling city of San Francisco seemed much farther away than that while standing in the middle of this ancient forest.

Two other towns were listed on the sign – Weott in ten miles and Myers Flat in seventeen. He thought that the campground was somewhere near Weott, so he wasn't far from the end of his day.

Only a couple of miles later he rolled into an unlisted town of Redcrest. Though it was little more than a wide spot in the road, it was still strange to see a town in the middle of the forest. But Redcrest was big enough to have a post office and a restaurant, so Mike decided to stop for a late lunch/early dinner. He was happy he didn't have to rely on the freeze-dried supplies he picked up this morning.

The restaurant was a casual affair with chairs and tables that looked like they were more at home in an office kitchenette from the 1970's. It was a compact room with maybe eight tables, but they weren't trying to impress anyone with the inside décor. The room had floor to ceiling windows separated with thin strips of metal. It provided the diners with a nearly unobstructed view of the forest and the main street of town, and it made the room feel much bigger.

Mike picked a bacon cheeseburger from the two-page, laminated menu. A burger always sounded good at the end of a ride, and this time he had no reason to talk himself out of the temptation. He didn't immediately pull anything out to read or work on and just enjoyed the serenity of the woods for a while.

The burger arrived shortly with fries and a large pickle, and the waitress dropped off a bottle of mustard and ketchup before disappearing into some hidden room in the back. He bit into the burger and it tasted wonderful. It was probably a very good burger in its own right, but things always tasted that much better when you were out on the road. It had also helped that he had been expecting noodle soup for dinner. He pulled out his thriller novel and read a couple of chapters as he took his time with the meal.

As far as he could tell, he was only eight miles or so from camp, and he still had hours before he had to worry about fading daylight. He did not need any dessert, but he decided he had time for a cup of coffee. The restaurant chair was not overly comfortable, but it was far better than a picnic table bench, so he settled in for another half hour of reading and coffee refills. He was happy to stretch out this day for as long as possible.

XIX

After lunch and coffee, he got on his bike once again to make the short journey to camp.

The numbers were beginning to pile up: miles, towns, pictures, climbing feet, wheel revolutions, burned calories, cups of coffee, etc. He had lost count of how many times he had remounted his bike, but he was pretty sure he would feel the bike seat imprint in his backside for weeks afterward. The remaining miles took less than a half an hour, so he was turning onto the camp entrance not long after his mind tuned out the narrow seat for the umpteenth time.

At first glance, the campground was little more than a place where the trees were less densely packed than other areas of the forest. It was likely that some of the trees had been cleared to make way for the camp, but it had been done in such a way that man's hand was not obvious.

The camp looked smaller than the ones he had stayed at so far, and he could see most of it from the main road just beyond a low, split-rail fence. There was less pavement as well, and this one seemed to be geared more toward tents than thirty-foot recreational vehicles. A campground just off the main road was usually to be avoided because of the traffic noise, but the Avenue of the Giants seemed to be a more sparsely traveled road.

Mike took a quick spin around the figure-eight shaped main road through the park. It looked like there were almost sixty sites, and only ten or so were occupied. There was one camper trailer toward the back, but the rest of the sites were occupied by tents. The tents were spread pretty evenly across the forest floor, so everyone had enough privacy to feel like they were nearly alone in the woods.

As he rode past the campers, he would give a nod of his head in greeting. It was a typical biker greeting, a friendly recognition that still allowed you to keep your hands on the handlebars. Most of the folks gave a quick wave in response, and the occasional smile.

After his lap around the figure-eight, Mike chose a spot near where the two loops intersected, thinking it would be quietest. The RV was some distance away, and it looked like the closest sites did not have children.

His closest neighbor had one of those Subaru Outbacks that had become very popular with the active set. A woman was unloading her gear from the rear hatch and gave Mike a smile with a laughing, perplexed look in her eyes, likely because this was the second time he had passed by in a couple of minutes. He returned her smile with a nod and a smile of his own.

He picked a site a few doors down the road and pulled his bike into the small turnout. Although the road through the campground was paved, the sites were not. The ground was covered with wood shavings and other forest debris, forming what looked like a very comfortable surface for a tent and sleeping bag. One site was barely discernible from another, and it was the most natural setting he had seen in a state campground.

The trees were definitely smaller than the giants he had seen earlier in the day, but some were still a few feet across at the base. There were a couple of tree stumps, but they were tall and jagged on the top indicating that the tree had met its demise in a way that didn't involve a chainsaw.

There were a few picnic tables strewn around, but they seemed communal rather than belonging to any particular campsite. There were also some concrete fire rings and a few bear boxes scattered across the forest floor. It was definitely a developed campsite but still felt more like a forest than anything else.

He returned to his bike and began unpacking his gear from the trailer. He picked a nice level spot far away enough from the base of a tree that he didn't see or feel any exposed roots. After putting up the tent, he threw some of his gear inside but didn't unroll his sleeping bag. He thought he might sleep outside tonight, depending on how his level of paranoia about forest creatures developed after the sun went down.

He had seen two bathrooms in his tour of the campground, and both seemed to have showers inside. He grabbed his chamois towel, bathroom kit and flip flops and walked to the nearest one. He hadn't exactly worked up a sweat over the last few hours, and it always seemed a little silly to wash up only to hang out in the woods, but he had become a creature of routine. It also helped him feel like he was stepping off the road for a while and helped him relax.

The path to the bathroom took him past the woman with the Subaru, and he was happy that she was not around this time. He didn't want to feel like a stalker. No need to inspire horror movie thoughts in anyone.

The showers were coin-operated like all the other ones he had come across. Of course, he had forgotten his new roll of quarters back at the campsite, but luckily there were still some loose coins in his toiletry kit. He hadn't been able to overcome the forgetfulness of his scattered brain, but he had tried to do certain things to outsmart himself. Stashing quarters in multiple places was one of them.

The water was just a step above lukewarm, so it wasn't the relaxing shower he had pictured in his head. It was also a bit hard to relax when there was a countdown timer ticking in your head. A few times when the water was closer to hot, he just sat under the shower until the three minutes expired. He then soaped up with the water off, deposited more money, and enjoyed another three minute blast of warmth while the soap rinsed away. This evening he showered quickly enough to come in under a single three minute cycle.

When he walked back to his site, he saw the Subaru gal again. She was moving things from her tent to the picnic table and did not initially see Mike walking up. She was probably in her mid-to-late thirties and looked to have an athletic build that matched the active lifestyle reputation of her Outback. Her brown hair was pulled back in a ponytail, and she was wearing a comfortable ensemble of a t-shirt, cargo shorts and all-weather sandals.

She turned as Mike passed by and offered him a more easy smile. Mike responded with a wave, a closed lip grin and a reflexive nod even though there was no longer a bike helmet on his head. Doesn't matter if you are single or married, a smile from a pretty girl will boost your spirits like nothing else does.

Back at his site, he draped his sink-washed clothing over the bent poles of his tent. There wasn't a lot of direct sunlight at this campsite, so it was unlikely the clothes would be much drier by sundown. The plastic bags that he packed his clothes in to protect them from the rain also came in handy to seal away damp clothes that hadn't had a chance to dry. He would probably build a fire later on, so maybe he could hang his bike gear nearby and speed up the drying process.

He didn't feel much like writing this evening, so he pulled out the guitar. He played with the strings quietly for a while but soon lost interest in that as well. He set it down on the picnic table and decided to stretch out on the ground. The forest floor was as comfortable as it looked, and he folded his hands behind his head and stared up at the trees.

He could not feel any wind at ground level, but the tops of the redwood trees swayed lazily back and forth in a gentle breeze higher up in the sky. The trunks of the trees were relatively clean of branches below the cap of green growth at the top, probably the only place where the sun hit the tree with any consistency in the dense forest.

The filtered sunlight gave the treetops a haloed glow and made them seem more magical than they already were. It felt like he was in some sort of enchanted forest from a fantasy novel, and the image was somehow relaxing. The combination of light and movement was a little hypnotic as well, and his mind drifted without entirely dozing.

"Would you like a beer?"

Mike blinked open his eyes, sat up on his elbows and saw Subaru girl at his feet. In one hand was a cold beer and in another a small cooler that probably contained a few more.

"Yes, yes I would" he replied. He rose a bit ungracefully as it didn't take long for his muscles to tighten up these days. If she had had a free hand, she might have taken pity and extended a hand to help him up.

"I saw you ride in on your bike and I figured you didn't have a cooler in that trailer of yours."

"No, I'm afraid not. Not really enough room, and I can't afford the extra weight. I'll sometimes pick up a six pack, but I have been skipping it the last few days.

She handed him a cold beer, set down her cooler on the picnic table, and then walked over to his bike. "That is quite the set up you have there. Not a lot of room, but it looks like you have most everything you need. Is it tough to tow behind the bike?"

Mike opened the beer by putting the edge of the bottle cap on the edge of the picnic table, and then slamming the cap with his left hand, popping it off the bottle.

"Nice trick," she said with another easy smile.

"Thanks. I'm Mike by the way."

"Erin," she responded and tilted her beer bottle toward Mike's. They clinked the necks together in greeting, and Mike raised his beer bottle as an additional toast before taking his first swig.

"Oh, that's good," he said after a long pull. "Actually, the trailer has been easier than I expected. It certainly slows me down on the hills, but I have gotten pretty used to it by now. Not a lot of room in it for the comforts of home, but I have plenty to keep me busy and out of trouble."

"How long have you been riding?"

"Overall, I've been on the road for about a week and a half. I started in Seattle and I'm headed to San Francisco. I suppose I'm about two thirds of the way there by now. "

"Whoa! That is quite the journey. So the obvious question is why?"

"Oh, I thought I'd take my mid-life crisis on the road. How about you? What brings you out to the middle of the woods?"

She frowned slightly when she heard his answer but let it pass. She responded, "Actually, I suppose I am doing the same thing, but in the opposite direction. I was an HR director for a tech company. Worked there for ten years, but when the stock dipped too low for comfort, they decided to lay off a bunch of people to show Wall Street that they were cutting costs."

She shook her head slightly as she continued, "I guess the stockholders get a warm fuzzy, but it left a lot of people out of work. Since I wasn't a programmer or some other crucial cog in the machine, my position was combined with another, and I was left out of the org chart."

"Well, that kind of sucks."

"It did, and it does. I'd been there for a long time and really believed in the company. But my story is hardly unique these days."

"Doesn't make it any easier," he sympathized.

"No, but it isn't the end of the world either. Although, I won't deny it felt that way for a while."

He paused and gave her a knowing smile. After a beat he asked, "So, now you're heading north?"

"Well, the job market is pretty brutal as you can imagine, and California is a little worse than average. I looked for work in my field for a few months, but there is really nothing out there. I received a decent severance package, and I have a little savings tucked away, so I decided to go back to school."

"What are you going back for?" Mike paused and smiled, "I mean, what are you going back to study?"

"I want to become a teacher. I know, not exactly a money maker these days, but it is something I am really interested in, and I am tired of thinking of only money. And jobs with big companies aren't exactly the safe havens they once were."

"No, no," he said putting up his hands in surrender, "I think that is awesome. I have a lot of respect for teachers. Actually, I have a couple of friends who teach. It sounds like it is difficult and frustrating at times, but they love it. And you can't argue with summers off."

"No, summers off will be pretty nice," she said with a smile. "I found a new program that allows people to go back to school in other states without paying the out-of-state tuition. Retraining the job force and all that. My parents actually live in Oregon, so that is where I am looking to go to school. I will probably stay with them until I find a part-time job. I am going to have to live pretty frugally from here on out. "

"Well, I think that is great. Most people wouldn't have the courage to make such a drastic change in both work and lifestyle. And to be an underappreciated teacher to boot. Good for you."

"Thanks," she said as she broke the conversational gaze and began walking around the campsite. "So I thought I would take the scenic route up to Oregon. I missed getting in for fall quarter, so I have some time to wander before being tied down with homework. Once I get registered and settled in, I'll fly back and drive up with the rest of my stuff. Hopefully, I will have my own place by then, but if not it will go into storage until I need it."

She walked past his tent and over toward the picnic bench. She set down her beer and picked up the guitar. "Was that you butchering the guitar earlier?" She wasn't facing him, but it sounded like she was smiling when she said it.

"Guilty. I'm afraid I only know two chords. I mostly just strum the thing and pretend it's music."

She turned to face him. "You're dragging a guitar down the west coast and you don't know how to play?"

"Yeah. I can't really explain it."

"Do you mind if I play?"

"Oh, please, go right ahead," he said with a wave. "The thing is going to waste in my hands."

She sat down on the top of the picnic table and put her feet on the bench seat. She set the guitar across her legs and started playing with the strings. She messed with the little white dials at the end of the guitar (he had no idea what they were called), leaned in and listened to the notes as she tried to get it tuned.

Mike said, "Well, see, if the guitar was in tune, I would have sounded a lot better."

Erin moved her eyes from the guitar to Mike's face without raising her head. The meaning of, "Seriously?" was pretty clear without any words.

"Yeah, you're right; I would just be butchering it in-tune."

She continued to work on the guitar, looking for a moment like she was done, before going back to tweak the strings again. Once she heard the tones she was looking for, she began strumming seemingly random notes, but they sounded like they blended quite nicely. After warming up for a bit, she moved right into an actual song, one Mike recognized but could not place.

While continuing to play she said, "So, I've told you my story. How about you tell me what you're really doing riding down the coast for two weeks?" She raised her head from the guitar and looked Mike straight in the eye. She had an expression that seemed to say, "Enough B.S."

For some reason, Mike was ready to tell his story. He wasn't sure if it was that enough time had passed, the remoteness of the woods, or simply that someone had not been satisfied with his pat answers. The directness of her question and expression seemed to break through his protective shell, and on some level he was a little relieved.

"How long do you have?"

"My social calendar is pretty free tonight," she responded with the smallest of grins.

"I think I'll need another beer. You want one?" She nodded yes, and he went to the cooler and grabbed two of the remaining four bottles. After slapping them open on the picnic table, he handed her a beer and sat down next to her on the picnic table top. It would be easier to talk if they were sitting side by side, and he didn't have to look into her eyes.

She continued to play the guitar softly, waiting patiently as Mike gathered his thoughts. He stared off into the woods at nothing in particular. In his mind he was rewinding through a series of images, wondering where to start.

XX

Mike began with a recap of how he and Katelyn had met, where they lived, what they did for a living, and other background information. He talked about how after losing his job, he had ventured off into something new, similar to what Erin was about to do.

While he was fast-forwarding through the background information, Erin continued to play songs that teased at Mike's mind to recognize, but that somehow seemed to encourage him along. Like a song playing in the background of a slideshow, the music added some additional depth and meaning.

"Over the past couple of years, particularly while I was struggling to get the business off the ground, there seemed to be this quiet resignation that things weren't going to be as great as we hoped. A feeling that we weren't going to live the quote/unquote American Dream. When we bought our house, we talked about how we would fix it up. We'd replace the dated kitchen, get rid of the old single pane windows, re-do the floors and all that. We'd put an addition over the garage for a master suite or a large family room. Things would just get bigger and better."

"But after I lost my job, we stopped talking about all those fun projects. Without ever saying it, I guess we were thinking that this is as good as it is going to get."

Erin stopped playing the guitar, maybe sensing that Mike was about to get into some deeper things and had gathered enough momentum to carry on without encouragement. She turned and set it behind their backs on the picnic table

Mike continued, "But then we started talking about having children. We had put off the decision for a long time, maybe waiting for some point where we felt financially ready. I think we both realized that point was never coming, so we just decided to go for it."

"Katelyn started reading all the books and taking all the vitamins. My work was finally treading water, and it looked like I could stop traveling so much. Katelyn made much better money, so I would be Mr. Mom and do some work on the side."

Mike paused for a long beat before continuing, "I was never drawn to kids much, but once I began picturing our own child, someone created from the two of us … all the doubts faded away. This was what it was all about, our own little American Dream."

"I started picturing trips to the park, play dates with other moms, dirty diapers and late night feedings. I hoped that I would be able to get some work done during nap time, but I was pretty stoked just to stay at home and be Dad. It was something I never imagined for myself, but soon it was all I was thinking about."

"I even went out and bought that trailer, even though I knew we wouldn't get to use if for quite a while. I found it used online, and had to have it. It was like this symbol of all I would do with our child. Oh, the places we would go."

Mike stopped talking for a while. He picked at the beer label of the bottle he hadn't been drinking. He stood up and walked around for a bit, shaking out his legs to get the circulation going again. Of course he was also stalling, wondering how much to share. But he had come this far, and it felt good to finally be talking. Erin just let him pace, allowing the silence to rest comfortably.

He walked back to the table and sat down next to Erin once again. He took a long pull on the beer before sighing his way into continuing.

"The first few months, nothing happened. I had no clue what the averages are for getting pregnant. Quite frankly, I had left most of the reading to Katelyn while I spent my time in la-la land, imagining life with our bundle of joy."

"It was interesting, Katelyn and I sort of switched places. I am usually the detail guy, reading every manual I can get my hands on while she spent time picturing the future."

"Though it was winding down somewhat, I was still traveling about every other week for three days at a time. Katelyn told me when prime baby-making-time was, so I would make sure I wasn't out of town at those points. But a couple more months passed by, and no baby."

"Katelyn stopped sharing interesting baby things she had found while she was reading, and I actually stopped seeing the books at all. She went from being enthusiastic to pessimistic, and sometimes seemed like she wanted to pick a fight. Then she would go through a bout of silence where she pulled back completely. I assumed that she was worried that we wouldn't be able to have kids, and she was just taking her stress out on me."

"We were still trying, but there seemed to be less 'this is the day, this is the hour' to the timing. I figured she was feeling overwhelmed and that she was trying to stop putting so much pressure on getting pregnant. As excited as I was to have a child, it was clearly stressing her out, so we kind of eased off for a while."

"For the next month or two, I kind of doubled up on the trips to meet vendors and potential clients. I was hoping that a strong push while I had the time would pay off later when our child was born. And taking a step back seemed to calm things down for Katelyn. She wasn't lashing out anymore, and just seemed more at ease. But I was also at home less, so there was this kind of awkward, disconnected feeling."

"I had a trip to Spokane the week before our anniversary, and I made reservations for a nice weekend away when I got back. I wanted to break out of the little funk we had fallen into. Start talking about the future again. Maybe our baby could even be conceived on our anniversary. It made some sort of cosmic sense in my head that this would be a great day to start things over."

"But we didn't need calendars or complicated anniversary conception plans. Katelyn was already pregnant when I got back from Spokane."

XXI

His trips had become frequent enough that it was just easier to leave his car in one of the satellite lots rather than have Katelyn pick him up at the airport. The shuttle bus picked him up outside baggage claim, and by the time they reached the lot, his car was idling out front ready to go.

He arrived at home around dinner time, the sun an hour above the horizon. Shadows stretched across the weathered lawn and crept up the walls of the house, providing too little shade against the setting sun. The west-facing windows acted like a magnifying glass, and the house baked under August skies each year.

The lawn was a crunchy, yellow brown, a blanket of neglect for all the neighbors to see. He had been gone too often lately to keep it alive through the single hot month of the year.

The driveway was empty, Katelyn probably having run some errands on the way home from work. Mike pulled into his spot in the driveway and shut off the engine. Neither of their cars was ever parked in the garage. Already lined with the implements of home ownership and ignored hobbies, the floor of the garage was now filled with chest high stacks of boxes.

Katelyn's parents had recently downsized to an apartment, leaving behind the cost and hassle of maintaining a house. It also meant that they didn't have the room to store all the things they had hung onto for years. Katelyn ended up taking not only the stuff from her own childhood, but many of her parent's mementos as well.

Mike had caught her out in the garage on several occasions just staring at the boxes. The generations had flipped, and she was now the keeper of the family history. She said she wondered how long it would be before all she had of her parents were these boxes. She seemed to be almost afraid of what she would find, and had yet to go through everything.

Mike pulled his suitcase out of the trunk and wheeled it up the sidewalk to the house. The entryway was the one sheltered spot on the front of the house, and it seemed especially dark after walking past the sunset glare of the windows. He thought to himself that he should put in one of those light sensors so the porch light would come on automatically when twilight arrived.

He opened the front door and the interior was similarly darkened and unnaturally quiet. He knew that Katelyn had not yet arrived, but his dog should have at least been there to welcome him home. But she was getting old, and maybe she was napping in the back and hadn't heard his car drive up.

Something else felt off, but he couldn't put his finger on it. The quiet seemed sudden, like a conversation interrupted.

He left his bag standing by the door rather than taking it to their bedroom. He went straight ahead into the living room rather than turning left to go down the hall. He couldn't shake the feeling that he was being watched, and it seemed safer to be walking through an open room rather than down a narrow hallway. He had probably been reading too many thriller novels lately.

He crossed through the living room without incident, and he rounded the corner into the dining room.

The kitchen was one of the things that first attracted them to the house. It was quite dated, with white Formica countertops and faded wood paneling on the cabinets. But it was spacious and the layout was good, and best of all it was completely open to the dining room. People always seem to gather in the kitchen when at a party, and this setup allowed people to hang out in the dining room and still feel connected to the activity of the kitchen.

He looked across the dining room into the kitchen, and he had an even greater sense that he had walked into a house that was a slightly-off copy of his own. Everything seemed to have been shifted three inches to the left.

His dog still hadn't come out to greet him, but of course he was moving as quietly as possible, and he hadn't flipped on any lights. Sensible or not, her continued absence made him worry even more about what had gone on. What might still be going on. He was thankful that he had arrived home before Katelyn.

The hallway entry into the kitchen was directly opposite the door to the office. He looked in without turning on the lights. Nothing seemed amiss, and the computer was still there as well as the other TV. Nothing missing, no one lurking.

He turned back into the kitchen and he saw a piece of paper on the counter that he had overlooked earlier. It stood alone on a completely cleared corner of the counter. His mind may have registered the empty space earlier when things seemed out of place, but had not locked in on the folded sheet of printer paper.

He saw his name written on it in Katelyn's handwriting and instantly felt a little silly for all the skulking around in his own house. She was probably just over at one of their friend's house for dinner and took the dog with her. He tossed his keys on the counter and turned to flip on the kitchen lights. It took a couple of flickers of the florescent lights to illuminate the room and to dispel his trumped up feelings of dread.

He walked down the hallway turning on more lights to chase away the shadows. After shutting the front door and flipping on the porch light, he turned the TV on low to have some background sound in the empty house. He returned to the kitchen, unfolded the note and read:

> I am not happy anymore. In fact, I am kind of miserable, and I think you have a lot to do with that. Your emotional distance has both pushed me away, and somehow dragged me down with you.
>
> Life is too short. I have found someone who makes me happy, so I want a divorce. Do not try to contact me.

I have retained a lawyer, and he will be contacting you in the next few days.

Also, I am pregnant. It is not yours. The dog is at Phillip and Lisa's. You can have the dog.

Katelyn

As he read the first line, the tension in his chest so briefly released, returned to grip his heart once more. A phantom hand grabbed his stomach and twisted it tighter and tighter as he read through the short note. His head began to wobble and he stumbled backward, dropping the note as his hands reached behind him trying to find a dining room chair. He watched the note flutter to the ground, for some reason expecting it to shatter when it reached the floor. Nothing so dramatic happened. It was just a piece of paper after all.

He felt like throwing up, but it was as if the knot in his stomach closed off any entry or exit to his stomach. He realized he had been holding his breath, and in a burst of release he began hyperventilating. His brain wasn't getting enough oxygen and there were starbursts firing across his vision. He bent his head over and looked at his hands, trying to focus on one thing like a drunken man might when he tried to stop the room for spinning.

He sat there, head down, staring at his wedding ring, willing the note away.

XXII

There on the picnic bench, he struck a similar pose. He was hunched over with his elbows on his thighs, staring past his feet at the ground below. His hands drooped at the wrist, and he was absentmindedly spinning his wedding ring with the thumb and index finger of his right hand. He went quiet.

Erin put her hand on his back but did not break the silence. At the touch of her hand, a switch was thrown inside of Mike and his back began to shake with wracking sobs. He remained almost entirely quiet as tears dripped off his bent face, dotting the picnic bench below. Erin remained silent but began rubbing her hand in soothing circles across Mike's back.

After a few minutes, Mike reached up to wipe the tears from his face without sitting up. Although he was pouring his heart out, for some reason he didn't want to show his face dampened by tears.

After wiping away most of the evidence, he sat up letting Erin's hand fall away from his back. He still wasn't quite ready to face her or hear any comforting words, so he spoke before she could. "I'm not sure how long I sat there in the kitchen, but by the time I snapped out of whatever state I was in, it was dark outside. I got up and walked through the rest of the house."

"Like I said before, nothing seemed different about the office, but that was basically my room. The next room down was a pseudo guest room, but it was really Katelyn's room. It was where she kept most of her clothes and stuff. I opened the door and it looked like we had just moved in. The dresser and futon were still there, but all of her clothes and jewelry were gone."

"Our bedroom was mostly spared, but her bedside table had been cleared off. I looked in the bathroom, and all her bottles of shampoo and conditioner were gone. The drawers where she kept her makeup and other gadgets were also empty. She had cleared out."

"I just kept walking through rooms, looking in corners, looking for something that wasn't there. When I got to the kitchen, I saw what hadn't clicked earlier. She had taken the fancy espresso machine and other things off the counter. The cords for her phone and headset were missing from the little charging station, and the tea she drank at night wasn't in the container by the stove. She had been pretty thorough."

"The living room hadn't changed much. All the furniture and electronics were still there. She had taken a few books from the bookshelves but had left all of our pictures behind. Not sure if they didn't mean anything to her anymore, or if she had left them behind to remind me of what I had lost."

Mike stopped talking again. After a minute of silence, Erin reached over and held his hand. Like the hand on the back, the small gesture let him know he wasn't alone. They sat there in silence for a while longer before Erin asked, "What did you do?"

"I got drunk."

Mike stood up, giving her hand a squeeze before releasing it and stood up. Snapping out of the world of his story, he realized that night was approaching in the woods just as it had at the house that night. There was also a slight chill in the air that he had been oblivious to, and an involuntary shiver rippled across his skin.

"I didn't realize how late it was getting. You still up for listening to my sob story?"

"It is hardly a sob story. I am ready to listen to whatever you want to share."

"We should probably build a fire. I haven't had a chance to stop by the office to buy any firewood. I can go do that now."

She said, "I am already stocked up at my campsite. Do you want to just move over there?"

"Sure. Let me just grab a couple of things."

He disappeared into his tent and for a moment he considered hiding in there until Erin gave up and walked away. After a brief internal debate about how much of an idiot he was, he came out with a sweatshirt and his headlamp.

He looked around the campsite to see if anything valuable was lying about. Of course, his bike was the most expensive thing, but his laptop and notebook would be the most painful to lose. The bike was already chained to one of the smaller trees, so he grabbed the backpack with his written and electronic notes and put its strap across his left shoulder. They walked in silence down the road to her campsite.

Her site was tidy but had all the trappings of a normal campsite. There was a propane stove at the end of the picnic table and a full size cooler on the ground underneath. Her tent was a taller version of his inaccurately labeled "four person" tent, and her boots sat on a little outdoor rug like a welcome mat by the door.

Her food was stored in the back of her Subaru, like a giant bear box safe from any scavengers. Mike realized that he hadn't stashed away his food yet, though it was all zipped up in the trailer. Hopefully it would be enough of a discouragement until he got back.

There were a few neat bundles of firewood sitting next to the concrete fire pit, tied together with green twine. Trying to feel somewhat useful, he offered to get the fire going. "Do you have a lighter and some paper for a fire?"

"There are a couple newspapers on the passenger seat, and a lighter near the stove. Have at it." She disappeared into her own tent, he assumed to change into something a little warmer.

He went to the unlocked car to grab the newspapers. It was a little odd how comfortable they were with each other already when they were essentially strangers. She seemed unconcerned leaving him alone or letting him go through her car. Actually, it was only odd when he looked back on it. Unexamined, it felt completely natural at the time.

He did not snoop, but there were things in his immediate sight that fleshed out the picture of who she was. The car smelled of vanilla but it was subtle. There was a coffee cup in the cup holder, but not the pile of fast-food bags that would accumulate in his car when he was on a road trip.

CDs were strewn on top of the newspapers on the passenger seat within easy reach so she could change out music while driving. He didn't recognize all of the bands, but they all seemed to be current. No music from the eighties or nineties as far as he could tell. The newspapers were from towns south of here, and they were a little travel journal of where she had been. The top one was a newspaper from Fort Bragg, a town a couple of days south on his own route.

He pulled the newspapers out from under the CDs letting them slide on to the seat. He found the lighter just where she said it would be and took it with him to the fire pit. There was a large, blackened metal grill attached to the concrete ring on two hinges. He swung it away expecting a loud creak, but the grill pivoted silently. Next to the split firewood was a bundle of kindling that would catch more quickly. No need to forage in the Redwoods for even the smallest twig.

He crushed a few pieces of newspaper into tight spheres and placed them on the bed of old ashes. Next he formed a tent of the smaller branches above the newspaper. He lit the edges of the newspapers and let them burn for a bit. Once they had caught, he added in some more loosely packed paper that would burn more quickly.

The higher flames caught the twigs, and once things were burning nicely he added in the pieces of split wood. Soon he had it going to the point where it would sustain itself unattended for a while.

He looked up and realized that Erin had moved some things from the back of the car and put them on the picnic table. There was a lantern in the center, and she had spread out some snacks. There was also a bottle of red wine and some plastic wine glasses.

He was looking over the spread as she came up behind him and said, "I'm not all that hungry, but I thought you might want to snack on something. I have a steak we can split if we get hungrier later. Can I get you another beer, or would you like a glass of wine?"

"I'll have whatever you're having."

"Well, I think I am ready to switch to wine. I don't think I want to hold onto a cold beer after the sun goes down."

"Wine sounds great. Thanks."

While she was opening the bottle, he grazed through the snacks she had put out. There was a selection of pre-sliced cheeses shrink wrapped from a deli counter, a jar of peanuts, and a container of hummus with some pita chips. "This is a pretty good selection for camp food. I can only imagine the spread you would put out at home."

She handed him a glass and said, "Oh, it isn't much fancier at home. It would be in nicer dishes though."

"Well, it looks great. Thanks again." He raised his glass to her, and they clinked them in a toast. Or rather they clunked them together as the glasses were plastic.

They lingered a while at the table, grazing on the snacks, caught between idle chatter and what they had been talking about earlier. Mike turned away first and walked over to the fire ostensibly to tend to it. He used one of the longer twigs as a poker and pushed the wood around the pit. Once he had messed with it sufficiently, he put another log on.

"So, you ready to talk again?" Then she smiled and added, "No pressure."

"If you're willing to listen."

"Carry on."

"Where was I?"

"I believe you were drunk," she prompted.

"Yeah. So I found the note, walked around the house, and found all the holes where her stuff used to be. I left my suitcase by the door and got in the car and drove. I had no clue where I headed, but I had to get out of there fast. It felt like the walls were closing in on me."

"I drove aimlessly for an hour or so. My mind was … well, I don't remember much of anything. At some point I ended up at the liquor store for bourbon and a convenience store for a bottle of Coke. I poured half the bottle of Coke on the ground and filled up the space with Jack Daniels. I drove out to West Seattle and parked along the strip by the beach."

Mike had been staring into the fire while he talked. He looked up and saw that Erin was standing directly across from him. There was a look of concern on her face, but she gave him a little nod to go on.

"On the north side of West Seattle there is a place called Alki Beach. It's a popular place, and the sidewalks are packed whenever it is sunny. The main road has the beach on one side and houses and shops on the other. A lot of the old houses have been knocked down for condos, but there are still these run-down beach houses stuck in between."

"I walked along the road for a while, drinking. It was dark and it was just me and the occasional dog walker. I walked to the point and back, but eventually I took off my shoes and wandered down to the water. I sat in the sand and just stared at the ocean."

"Images kept popping up and I would feel an almost a physical stab of pain. Everything I had done. Everything I hadn't done. All the times I held back and didn't reach out. All the little things I did to push her away. I was shouldering all the blame at that point. I hated myself."

"I don't know how long I stewed, but eventually I got up and walked back to the road. It may have been a subconscious thing, but I had stopped across the street from where a friend lived. I walked into the building, but instead of going to his apartment, I headed up on the roof. He had had a bunch of parties, and we always ended up on the roof to look at the water and the lights of downtown."

Mike paused again and took a sip from the glass of wine. It was almost empty at that point, though this was the first sip he remembered taking. When he looked up from the fire, he realized that Erin had made her way around the fire pit and was standing next to him. He looked into her eyes and he could see the fire flickering in them. He also saw compassion rather than pity. She took his hand once again and then turned away to face the fire. In a low voice she asked, "And then?"

"Well, my bottle was empty at that point, and I was pretty drunk. I went through the door and out on to the roof. The surface of the roof was wet, and it reflected the lights of the city. It seemed to stretch right out into Puget Sound."

"At that point my mind flipped from blaming myself to thinking about Katelyn cheating on me. I didn't know if the pregnancy line was true or just an extra twist of the knife, but I couldn't stop imagining her with someone else. And I kept walking toward the edge of the roof." He felt Erin's hand tighten around his.

He continued on, "I have this rather unusual fear of heights. It isn't even a fear exactly. I have this almost primal feeling that I need to jump. I can almost feel the hand on my back pushing me along, and I have to dig in my heels when I get near an edge. That night I just plowed ahead, right up to the little half wall that ran along the edge."

"I was despondent, angry, jealous, sick…I was out of my head. And I was scared because my body wasn't resisting the pull of the edge. The urge to jump had never been suicidal. It was something different, like I wanted to see what would happen. But that night, my mind wasn't talking my body out of jumping. If I had stepped up on that wall right when I first walked up, I don't know that I would have stopped. "

"After a minute of leaning out over the edge with the top of the wall digging into my thighs, I couldn't take it anymore and I turned around and sat down hard on the roof. The lights disappeared and the roof became inky black."

"I sat there staring at the darkness, trying to calm down. I didn't want to stand up until I was sure I would walk back down the stairs. I sat there for a long time, letting all the shitty images wash over me again."

"I'm not sure how long I sat there, but the water on the roof had soaked through my pants and I was shivering. I sat there until a single thought came into focus that I knew would get me back down off that roof."

"What was it?" she asked.

"I would like to say that it was God, family, friends, or even hope that pulled me back. Those will eventually help pull me out of the tailspin, but I was a long way from thinking clearly. The simple thought was that the wall had saved me. It was this low wall on the roof that gave me time, a chance. It stopped me from doing something I couldn't come back from."

"For all the walls I used to shut myself off, a wall ends up saving me. I could feel the universe laughing."

"I was in the middle of my own little shit storm, but I thought that once I got back down on solid ground and sobered up...well, this sort of stuff happens every day, right? Maybe I could laugh *with* the universe someday."

"I finally made it down the stairs, walked across the street, picked up my shoes and walked back to the car. When I got there, I threw the keys in the trunk, got in the passenger seat, pushed it all the way back, and tried to go to sleep. I stared at the roof liner for a while, but eventually the booze took over, and I passed out."

As soon as he finished his story, Erin took his other hand and turned him around to face her. Without a word, she took him in a firm hug, cupping the back of his head with her hand. He did not cry this time, but he felt his body release the tension he had held onto for so long.

XXIII

They stood there by the fire, holding onto each other. She would occasionally whisper things like, "I'm glad you came back down" and "you are going to make it through this". They swayed slightly like teens awkwardly getting through a slow dance.

He took a number of deep breaths, trying to physically expel the remaining tension and pain. A feeling of relief swept through him that left him feeling ten pounds lighter.

After a particularly deep breath, he squeezed her tightly and said, "Thank you." He pulled away from the hug, meeting her gaze briefly before turning away. He backed away a step or two and turned to the fire for something to do.

He knelt down and rearranged the burning logs as he continued. "So, anyway, I woke up early the next morning, fortunate to have been ignored by Seattle's Finest during the night. I got the keys out of the trunk and drove a few blocks to a coffee shop. I was pretty nauseous but I felt like I needed to get something in my stomach to soak up the alcohol."

"I sat there thinking about what had happened, and the empty house I would go back to. I wasn't ready to face my friends or family. I mean, what was I supposed to tell them? I knew I had to get out of town for a while, just like I knew I had to get out of the house the night before. The guilt, the shame … the weight of everything … I just had to get out."

He told her about Gerry and his own ride down the coast. It seemed like exactly what Michael needed at that moment. Go where no one knew what he was going through. He didn't have to function in society, and he could be overwhelmed and not care about who saw him.

He told her how he hoped that all the time on the road would help him sort things out in his mind, and he could punish himself physically for the pain and guilt tearing him up inside. That he hoped that by following through on at least one thing that he had planned but put off, that it would somehow start him down the right path.

Leaving Alki, he went home, showered and took his bike into the shop for a quick tune up, pleading his case to get it back that afternoon. He called the couple who was watching their (his) dog and asked them if they could take care of her for another couple of weeks. He told them that it was a family emergency but didn't go into the details. He was sufficiently upset on the phone that they didn't press it any further.

He dug out the paperwork Gerry had given him about the ride and looked through it to see what to expect. He went out and bought travel-sized bottles of stuff, large plastic bags to keep his clothes dry, and a notebook. He told Erin that he had been writing most nights on the way down and that he thought it was helping somewhat.

After picking up his bike from the shop, he went back home to pack. He pulled the trailer out of the hiding place in the shed and loaded it with his camping gear, clothes and backpack. He attached the trailer to the bike and took it for a spin. It was only a mile or so, but it was enough to give him an idea of how it would track behind the bike.

When he pulled the bike/trailer combo into the garage, he saw the guitar leaning in the corner. On impulse, he wedged it into the trailer. The neck stuck out but he supposed it made it clear he wasn't towing children.

When he went back in the house, the note was still on the dining room floor where he had dropped it the night before. He picked it up, put it back on the counter, and slept on the couch.

"A week and a half later, here I am."

"So, how are you feeling now?

"I still feel like shit of course. I'm no Catholic, but I embrace guilt with the best of them. I have been replaying all the times over the years that I didn't say what I felt. How I pulled into my own little miserable shell and did nothing to show how much I loved her. I can't forgive her for what she did, but at this point I am still kind of wallowing in my own failures."

"As brutal as it has been to lose Katelyn, and imagine the details of her betrayal, the thing I have been thinking most about is the child we will never have. I can still picture his little face. It is so vivid. It feels like a punch in the gut every time I see it."

He paused before going on, "I can look at myself as a failure, and chalk her up as a dishonest cheater, but the kid just seems like an innocent bystander caught in the crossfire. And now he's just, gone."

After another long pause, he looked up again at Erin and said, "I know that I am running away. Running from the pain and having to deal with the aftermath. But it still feels like this trip was the right thing to do. I don't think any of it makes any better sense yet, but I think that this time on the road will help me when I go back to face it."

Erin hugged him once more. It was less intense this time, like she had been tailoring the embraces to his needs, and felt that he was now farther back from the abyss.

She broke the embrace and stepped back. She extended her right hand out with the palm facing up, and looked into his eyes. She said, "I think it is time."

He stared back at her, not knowing what she meant at first. Then he understood.

He spun his wedding ring three times, and then took it off and placed it gently in the center of her palm.

Her fingers closed over the ring, but she did not lower her hand. They sat in silence for a moment before she asked, "Would you like some company tonight?"

His eyes moved up from her closed fist to the trees above their heads. He stared at the branches lit up by the dying fire and tried to take in all that had happened in the last few hours since she had appeared at his feet. This night had been incredible for him, and he did not want it to end. But he was still so confused.

After futilely looking to the sky for the answers, he lowered his head and met her gaze. "I would. But … I …"

She held up her empty left hand and said, "Just company, nothing else. You can just be here to protect me from the bears."

He smiled and said, "OK. I could do that."

"All right then. I am going to pack up the food and get some water to douse the fire. You go get your sleeping bag and pillow, and I will meet you back here."

She paused, and then continued in a lower voice, "I am going to put your ring in your backpack. I don't want you tossing it in the fire or chucking it in the woods. I know this ring still means something to you, and you will know what to do with it sometime down the road."

He met her gaze again, this time with tears beginning to well up. He opened his mouth to say something more, but all he could manage was "Thank you."

"You're welcome," and then in a more marching-orders tone, "Now go get your stuff."

He pulled his headlamp out of his pocket, put the strap around his forehead and started walking off into the darkness.

After he had left, she went to his backpack and placed the ring in one of the outside, zippered pockets. She also pulled out his journal. There was a pen clipped into the spiral wire along the side, and it looked weathered with bent over corners.

She flipped through the pages without really reading them. He had filled it about halfway so far, and she took that as a good sign. She paused at the last page for a long moment before returning the notebook to his backpack.

While Mike was at his own campsite, he put his food in a bear box and threw the rest of his loose gear into his tent before grabbing his pillow and sleeping bag. The two bottles of beer and glass of wine had made it through his system, so he stopped by the bathroom before heading back.

By the time he returned, she had cleared away all the food and filled a large container of water to douse the fire. She had begun spreading out the remaining coals, but had left the fire lit so there was a beacon for him to follow.

When he walked into camp, she took his sleeping gear from him and said, "I'll set up the tent while you put out the fire." She turned from him and as he watched her walk away, he thought to himself, "How in the world did I get here?"

He slowly poured the water on the glowing coals, and a plume of steam rose into the air with a loud whoosh. He let the air clear and stirred the coals again before hitting them with another shot of water. After the third dousing, he turned off his headlamp and there were no remaining embers glowing in the pit.

He stared up at the sky again. Now that the campfire was out, the stars were more easily seen through the branches. He was reminded once again that there was so much beauty in the world. We just can't always see it.

He flipped on his headlamp again and did a quick scan of the campsite. It didn't look like anything of value or resembling food had been left out. Then he walked over to Erin's tent. He could see a light glowing but no shadows were moving across the fabric walls. "Knock, knock," he said when he reached the door. He was feeling rather awkward all of the sudden.

"Door's open," she replied.

He unzipped the tent flap and peered in. There was a battery powered lantern at the far end of the tent, and he saw his backpack among her bags in one corner. She had unzipped both bags so that one was a base and one was a blanket. It looked like she had another multi-colored, Mexican style blanket that she could throw on top if it grew cold.

"Come in, you're letting in all the cold air," she joked. She was tucked in on the left side of the bed and all he could see was the top of her head poking out from under the covers. He kicked off his shoes and stepped inside. He stood crouched in the corner looking down on Erin. He, again, felt a bit awkward. "Uh, I didn't exactly bring pajamas with me. All right if I take off my shorts?"

"As long as you keep your skivvies on, I think we'll be fine."

He pulled off his shorts and climbed in under the covers. She was wearing a t-shirt and what looked like running shorts. When their feet touched, he noticed she was also wearing socks for warmth. She rolled up on her elbow to face him, so he did the same. She had pulled her hair out from its ponytail and it fell just past her shoulders. He shouldn't be thinking this way, but she really was quite beautiful.

Her eyes that were playful earlier grew serious as she gazed at his face. She seemed to be at relative ease, and his awkwardness fell away. She took her right hand and placed it on the side of his head. She said, "Your story was painful, but I am glad you told me. It doesn't seem like it now, and you probably won't believe me when I say this, but it will get better."

He replied, "Thank you, for everything you've done tonight. I still feel lost, but just saying it all out loud for the first time..."

He looked down for a moment to gather himself, and then said, "Trying to explain it to you has helped somehow."

"You're welcome." She slid her hand down and took a hold of his left hand. She then rolled over onto her right side, taking his left hand with her, and pulling him into a spooning position. He scooted over so their bodies were touching from head to toe. She clasped his left hand and brought it up to her chest just under her chin. They took a few deep breaths together before settling into a calming rhythm.

He felt safe and maybe even loved for the first time in weeks.

And he slept soundly.

XXIV

He awoke the next morning, alone again.

The trees filtered all but the noon day sun, so the tent would remain shaded for much of the day. He was unsure of the time, but it was likely still early as the air temperature was quite cool. He had slept well, though his dreams were troubling. They were mostly a series of images with little connection, but there was a sense of doom lurking behind them.

He rolled over onto his back and stared up at the top of the tent. The previous night returned to him slowly – seeing Erin standing over him when he was stretched out flat, the guitar, the fire, all he had talked about, all he had shared, all she had done to hold him up, and the shelter of her bed. A fraction of a smile flickered across his face.

In the background of his little morning flashback, there was the smell of coffee.

He rolled over onto his stomach and pressed himself into standing. He was a little unsteady on his feet, but he managed to get dressed without falling over. He rolled up his sleeping bag and set it on end with his pillow balanced on top. He grabbed his backpack, unzipped the tent flap and walked out into the morning.

Erin was sitting on the top of the picnic table with her elbows resting on her thighs. She had tied her hair back again and had put on a sweatshirt and pants. She had a cup of coffee pressed between her palms and was rolling it back and forth slightly. There was steam coming from the top of the cup, so the coffee was fresh. Her eyes seemed to be looking through the steam at some sort of phantom. She raised her eyes to look at Mike and simply said, "Good Morning."

Her face was hard to read initially. Though nothing really happened, did she regret inviting a stranger into her tent? Was this some sort of awkward morning after, and she just wanted to send him home quietly on a walk of shame? Was he just paranoid and imagining rejection out of reflex now?

As if reading his mind, she smiled and said, "Don't worry. No need to feel awkward. Nothing happened to feel guilty about. No regrets for my part."

Letting a puff of breath out he said, "I'm glad to hear that. I was just going over the evening in my mind, and it is still a little hard to believe. After being knocked flat with pain, guilt and self loathing, you show up at my feet, haloed in sunlight like an angel. And with beer no less."

She chuckled, "Well, I'm no angel, but you do paint a lovely picture of me this morning." She gestured over her left shoulder, "There's coffee on the stove and I've got some day-old cinnamon rolls in the back of the car if you're hungry."

"Coffee sounds great." He walked over to the stove, and there was a Styrofoam cup there waiting for him. He poured the coffee from the percolator, and it looked nice and strong. He came back around to stand in front of her before continuing.

"Well, angelic pictures aside and without being overly dramatic, you were there for me in a way that I can't begin to repay. I have been trying to sort this all out, alone in my head, and two weeks of reading and writing can't compare to a few hours of talking with you."

"I still don't regret taking off like I did, but you've made me realize that I am not going to get through this by myself. No matter how much I want it to be, this is not one of those 'pull yourself up by your bootstraps' kind of moments. So, a thousand times, thank you."

They clinked their coffee cups together. It was less a toast and more a sign of solidarity this morning. She drank out of her own cup with both hands and the effect was both innocent and sweet.

He continued, "I don't believe that everything happens for a reason, or that there is a grand plan that brings people together – but after last night, it is hard to argue that there isn't someone out there watching over me right now."

"All right, all right. Enough of the heavenly metaphors," she said with a smile. "But seriously, you cannot repay me for whatever hand I had in what happened last night."

She continued, "There are times when we all need a little help, and it can come from a dear friend or a stranger that we meet by chance. We can ascribe this chance meeting to destiny or randomness, but it doesn't really matter. What is important is what happens after we meet. Whether we reach out or not. And whether we are willing to accept the grace that is given. "

She stopped for a moment and stared at her cup of coffee. She seemed to be somewhere else, but Mike held off because it seemed like she wasn't finished.

After a long pause she continued, "What I mean by you can't repay me … someone helped me when I was going through a dark time in my life. He did much more for me than anything I have done for you. But by helping you, I am honoring him. Somewhere down the road, you will be there when someone reaches out, and in a way, I'll be there as well."

A feeling of warmth passed through Mike, and it wasn't just the coffee. It was a feeling of love in some way. Not a romantic feeling, but rather an intense feeling of appreciation, presence and wonder. The veil had dropped, the mask was removed, and there was clarity and connection.

He looked into her eyes and said, "Well, I hope I can do this moment justice someday."

"I have no doubt in my mind that you will," she replied. She dug around in her pocket and pulled out a slip of paper. She handed it to him and said, "This is my e-mail address. Let me know that you made it to San Francisco safely. And sometime farther down the line, let me know that you have found your way back."

He took the slip of paper from her and put it in his pocket. He could have lingered all morning, but this seemed to be the moment to say goodbye. "I will definitely keep in touch." He put down his coffee cup and took hers away. He took her hands in his and said, "I will never forget this."

She smiled and said, "You'd better not." She stood up and hugged him once more, then said, "Take care of yourself. Be safe." He squeezed her a little tighter and said, "I will," before letting her go.

Before turning away he continued, "You're going to be a hell of a teacher someday." She simply smiled in response.

He put his backpack on and walked back to the tent to grab his sleeping bag and pillow. He walked back to her, kissed her on the cheek and said, "Goodbye, Erin". He walked back to his campsite resisting the temptation to look back.

Nothing looked disturbed back at his campsite. He pulled everything out of the tent and broke it down quickly. He repacked his trailer, grabbed the food from the bear box and was ready to return to the road.

He decided to take the long way around the loop so he would not pass by Erin's campsite. It seemed like their moment together had finished neatly, and he did not want to disturb the ending.

He pedaled out of the campsite, leaving the guitar leaning against a tree.

XXV

His next stop was Fort Bragg some eighty miles away. According to the flight plan, he had four more days of riding before he would roll into San Francisco. For the first time, he was beginning to look forward to reaching the end of his journey.

The first fifteen miles of the ride were a continuation of the Avenue of the Giants, and once again he had the road almost entirely to himself. He replayed the night with Erin over in his mind, and there was a contented smile on his face as he passed beneath the canopy of trees. His heart felt at rest and seemed to be in tune with the peace of the forest. He knew that the pain would return, but for now the trees sheltered him from the outside world.

When the road rejoined Highway 101, and he left the state park, the hillsides cleared and the horizon opened. Though he had not passed into a town, it was still an abrupt feeling of returning to civilization. There were a couple of long hills soon after, and they helped break any remaining spell that had taken hold in the forest.

As afternoon pressed in to replace morning, his growling stomach reminded him that he had not had much of a dinner the night before. He found a roadside store and stopped in to find something to eat. Throwing nutrition to the wind, he bought a box of chocolate glazed mini donuts to go with a cup of coffee, and went outside to eat his meal of caffeine and sugar in the sun.

The store looked more like a house than a convenience store, and it had a large covered porch out front. There were no comfortable chairs to sit on, so Mike sat on the edge of the porch and let his legs dangle over the side.

Over the past hour, the road had slowly climbed through a series of undulations and in and out of some smaller state parks. After the brief exposure, he was back among the trees. He stared at the canvas of green across the street and let his mind wander.

He thought about why it was the loss of their child that had dominated his mind over the past week. Why was he more upset about losing something he had imagined than what he actually had?

As he had told Erin, part of it was that the child was innocent. He was just out there, waiting for Michael and Katelyn to get their act together. But because they were weak, because they failed, the child would never have a chance to even exist. Collateral damage in a pointless battle.

But it was more than that. Over the past few months as they readied themselves to be parents, Michael found passion and excitement he hadn't felt in a very long time. He was making plans again. Believing.

The child was the hub that the new world would revolve around. As this new world began to take shape in his mind, the face of his imagined son came into clearer focus. The little boy was a sign of hope, a possibility of renewal, a chance for a future with some meaning. A future Michael had counted on, because he had made his present so miserable.

He had clung to that vision while ignoring the signs that his marriage was falling apart. He had kept his renewed excitement mostly to himself while Katelyn drifted away, finding passion somewhere else.

The little boy had become Michael's future. Now that future had been ripped away, and somehow that was the hardest thing.

~

Continuing on, he passed through the town of Leggett and turned to take Highway 1 toward the coast.

He had been on 101 for three states and more than five hundred miles. Highway 1 would take him all the way into San Francisco, so ninety percent of his trip was on just two roads. The cue sheets had been pretty detailed, but he supposed the turn-by-turn directions could have been condensed to a single sheet for the thousand mile trip.

Not long after joining Highway 1, the road climbed again in earnest. It was a two-lane road that twisted and turned up the edge of the hillside, and he couldn't see more than a few hundred feet before the road disappeared around another corner. The trees grew close to the roadside further blocking the view ahead, and there wasn't much of a shoulder on either side of the road. Even the air seemed compressed and it felt like the forest was closing in to consume him.

He pushed back.

He pressed hard against the forces closing in on his mind as he leaned into the hill before him. There were few cars taking this shortcut to the coast, so he was free to take the road for much of the climb. He stood out of the saddle and danced on the pedals like he was a pro taking on the fabled Alp d'Huez. He was able to white out his mind with the hard effort, and soon all that was left was the chant, "Don't. Crack! Don't. Crack!" repeated over and over in rhythm with his pedal strokes.

He climbed more than 1,200 feet over three miles, reaching the summit at almost 2,000 feet. It was quite literally the highest point of the trip, and it was quickly followed by one of the biggest highlights of the trip.

After cresting the hill, the road followed an equally twisting path down the other side. The way down was not as steep as the climb, but it went on forever. He coasted through turn after turn, braking on the way in and then shooting through the apex on his way to the next one. The road was heavily shaded, and the only sounds he could hear were the whizzing gears and the occasionally squeaking brakes bouncing off the chute of trees.

The trees began to thin as he rode farther down the hillside, and without the shade he began to warm up even in the rushing wind. After an incredible twelve mile downhill ride, the hillsides finally receded completely, and after one last left turn he was back out at the ocean. The silence of the forest was replaced by the roar of the surf crashing into the shore. It was an incredible path out of the darkness and into the light. From the enveloping trees to the endless horizon of the ocean.

The road turned south but bent inland almost immediately. Soon he was headed up another five hundred foot hill. Just when he thought he was coasting along on level footing, another obstacle presented itself.

For the next twenty miles, Highway 1 hugged the coastline and Mike was carried along by a firm tailwind. He was really sailing now with the helping hand on his back, and he arrived at the campground less than an hour later. His spirits were buoyed by the ease of the speed and the wonderful views of the ocean.

The campground was a few miles north of the town of Fort Bragg and just a short walk away from the ocean. He found an empty campsite on the western side of the grounds, somewhat protected from the onshore winds by a raised berm. He had seen a Mexican restaurant right by the camp entrance, so he decided he was eating out this evening.

Once he had set up his tent, he changed into flip flops and headed down to the beach. The trail took him up and over the berm, and there was a paved path heading north-south along its crest. He guessed it was a bike path into town.

The beach on the other side was not as welcoming as most he had seen. It was rather steep and rocky, and the water churned menacingly in the small cove. He stuck his feet in but didn't venture too far out.

As was his habit, he stared out at the horizon and let his mind drift. The peace he had found earlier in the day dissipated as he thought about Katelyn, their marriage, the note, the house, children, whether she was really pregnant, and what he had done to make her so hateful in the end. He had spent much of the trip down looking at his own faults and mistakes, but now all the images were awash in hues of anger.

How could she just cast him aside without so much as a conversation? How could she betray him and their marriage vows? How could she have cheated? How long had she lied? How could she have ripped away their future? How could she have taken away their child?

As he came back around from the angry images in his head, he realized he had been hurling rocks out into the ocean. He had no idea how long he had been at it, but his arm hurt from the effort.

As he calmed down and continued to come back to the present, he was thankful that he had not been wearing his wedding ring. He easily could have thrown it into the ocean without ever seeing it go.

When he was fully back, he noticed that the sun was still quite high in the sky. He decided to get cleaned up and see if that path went into town. He quickly showered and changed into street clothes. He walked his bike up the berm to the path and started pedaling south. It was a little awkward pedaling with normal shoes, but it was more uncomfortable to walk around in bike shoes. So, it was a decent trade off for the short trip into town.

The path took him right into town, and he rode down the main drag for a mile or two. He briefly considered staying in town for dinner, but he already had his mind set on the Mexican restaurant. It was within walking distance to his campsite, and that appealed to him somehow.

He was a little hungry, but it was too close to dinner for a full meal, so he decided to stop at a coffee shop for a cup o' Joe and something sweet. He found a table near the window and pulled out his notebook to do some writing. After talking with Erin the night before, thoughts had been cascading rapidly through his mind, and he needed to get them down on paper.

His pen could not go fast enough to keep up with his mind. He wrote furiously, making short notes in the margin if something random came to mind that he couldn't get to right then. By the time his thoughts slowed to a trickle, two hours had passed.

He had always wanted to be a writer, and often imagined being so passionately caught up in a story that everything else fell away.

He never imagined it would be his own story that grabbed him so strongly, or that the destruction of his marriage would be the topic. Unfortunately, he had to write what he knew (or at least what he was experiencing).

He pedaled back into camp, ditched his bike, grabbed his headlamp and book, and started walking to the Mexican restaurant. The road was nicely wooded, and the sound of the ocean began to retreat after a few hundred feet. His mind was almost equally quiet. He had dumped quite a bit out on the page, and he tried to fill in the void with the sights and smells of the woods before anything else could sneak back in.

The restaurant was nondescript from the outside. There were no pseudo-adobe walls, exposed red beams or decorative cacti outside to lure people in from the road. Inside, it was a little more confusing.

The red and white checkered plastic table cloths and the dangling white lights made it feel more Italian. However, there were piñatas hanging from the ceiling and the walls were covered with an explosion of Mexican curios to ensure you had not been duped by the sign outside. It was as if they had gone through a couple of different menus already and were keeping their options open in case this iteration was not successful.

The length of the building ran right to left from the entrance, and Mike saw a small bar off to the right. He decided to eat in there as the dining room was nearly full already. He found a seat and took a look at the menu after ordering the requisite margarita on the rocks. The menu was not much different from any other Mexican restaurant, but he didn't consider that a bad thing. He was in the mood for comfort food, not to be dazzled by the inventiveness of the chef.

When his drink arrived, he ordered some enchiladas and took out his book to read. He had chosen to sit at one of the tables, as the actual bar was nearly full. There were three girls and one guy at the bar already, and they appeared to be all together. He decided not to take the one remaining stool and intrude on their party.

Although they were together, it appeared that the guy did not know all of the women. It was not clear where he fit in, but he wasn't letting that stop him. He was talking about the most inane topics, seemingly fishing for some commonality to work his way in and set the hook. It also appeared that he had not decided who he was pursuing yet. He was trying to work all three, even though one had on a wedding ring.

It depressed Mike on multiple levels. Was this the sort of guy that had lured Katelyn into betraying her marriage vows like some car salesman trying to close a deal? Had she gone out trolling herself with a group of women? How many of her friends knew about all this, or even helped her along? How many people knew before he did?

And almost as depressing, was this what his future held, talking gibberish in a desperate attempt not to go home alone?

Although his eyes scanned over the pages of his book, he retained absolutely nothing. He kept turning back to the beginning of the chapter to start over, but even on the third pass his eyes were working independently of his brain. The words on the page were unable to keep the depressing images of the barflies out of his mind.

When his dinner arrived, his stomach was sufficiently twisted up that he was no longer hungry, and the margarita had gone sour. He picked at his dinner long enough to finish half of it because he knew that his body needed it. Before he left, he had them pack up the leftovers in case he felt like eating later. The guy at the bar seemed to be getting somewhere, although maybe he was getting worked as well.

Night had fallen outside, so he put on his headlamp and aimed it down the road back to camp. The trees were darkly outlined against the barely lit sky. It might have been beautiful, but he did not see it right now. Depression seemed to do that – block out the rest of the world, making sure that you saw only the thing you felt worst about.

His eyes followed the little circle of light dancing ten feet in front of him, while his mind churned through more painful thoughts.

XXVI

The next couple of days passed by quickly. Gerry's group had stayed in Fort Bragg for their second day off, but Mike didn't feel like sticking around for any length of time. San Francisco was now in his sights, and he wanted to keep pressing forward.

Highway 1 hugged the coastline, climbing high above the crashing surf, and the morning was one continuous scenic overlook. For most of the first day, the coastline was broken up by narrow canyons that had been slowly carved by rivers emptying into the sea.

At each canyon, the road would dip inland for a mile or so to reach a narrower crossing, and then climb back out to the coast. The climbs out of each crevasse were relatively short but very steep. On one of them he was out of his seat, throwing his weight into the lowest gear, and barely maintained enough speed to avoid tipping over.

There were no major towns along the route, so when he did stop, it was often at an offbeat little café or coffee house. The pace of the people seemed to be in tune with the size of the town, and it made him pause and linger even with the light pressure at his back to continue.

He began to replay his trip in his mind to distract himself from thoughts of the days preceding it. The individual days of the trip had already begun to blend together in his mind, and he was glad that he had taken what few pictures he had. He was also thankful that he been writing most nights as well.

Along with his travel notes, his notebook was a piece of his recovery. He had not come up with any answers, but he knew that he had made the first painful steps in the right direction. The next big one would be to face his friends and family with the news.

And in his mind, it did feel like he was facing them, a panel of people who would judge him for what he was about to reveal. Many of them had stood up there with him when he married Katelyn on that autumn day, and he felt like he had let them down as well. It didn't matter whether they felt that way or not, his sense of failure was large enough to project these feelings onto his friends' faces.

He was dreading having to tell the full story, face to face with someone who not only cared for him, but Katelyn as well. It still loomed large in his mind, but the night with Erin had helped. The dry run with a stranger gave him a sliver of confidence that he could make it through the telling.

For as much doubt he had running through his head, there was very little second-guessing about this trip. The trip was born of an unquestioned impulse, something he never allowed himself, and for once he did not rehash the ramifications of the decision.

When he read the note and realized the life he had known had come to an end, he ran. Not exactly a long term solution, but he was glad he had stepped away for a moment. He did not pretend that the shit pile waiting for him at home was going to be any smaller or less rank for having ignored it for two weeks, but he felt like he had now at least armed himself with a shovel.

~

The next day was more of the same – small towns and spectacular scenery at the seeming edge of the world.

Morning mist hung on the coastline as he climbed the hills in almost complete solitude. He was glad that most people now chose to drive along the wide freeways farther inland, and left the twisting, cliff-side highways to the more aimless wanderers. As if to punctuate the more remote feel, there were cattle guards across the highway in seven different spots. Rolling over the open grids made his hands shake and teeth chatter under the warm sky.

Farther down the road, he saw birds drifting upward on a warm column of air. As he rode closer, he realized they were turkey vultures circling over a specific spot. "Sorry guys. I'm not dead yet," he thought to himself as he rode past.

The route for day twelve would take him inland off Highway 1 and stop less than thirty miles from San Francisco. It seemed silly when he had looked over the route a few years back, but now it made more sense.

The organizers had done a great job finding campgrounds spaced pretty evenly along the way, typically between 75 and 85 miles apart. The last two days could have been combined into one long day, but they knew that crossing the finish line would be more enjoyable at the end of a thirty mile day, rather than a hundred mile pedal. Mike did not plan on changing the script at the last moment.

The campground was another deeply forested affair and was relatively empty midweek. It dawned on him that this would be the last time he had to set up camp. Every night for nearly two weeks he had set up his tent only to break it down the next day. It had become meditative like any repetitive task can be. It was also somewhat cathartic to be able to set up home anywhere and depend on a much smaller number of things for comfort.

After setting up, he went to take a shower. As thankful as he had been for them each night, he would not miss the coin-operated showers. Beyond their cash determined brevity, it was very difficult to keep your clothes dry when you had to drag everything into the stall with you. He supposed he could have left his dry clothes out in the general bathroom area, but he had seen enough movies where someone walks off with your clothes as a joke to feel entirely comfortable. He skipped washing out his riding gear this evening with the promise of civilization and a Laundromat just a day away.

He had not stopped for any more food provisions either as he wanted to use up what he already had. Tonight's dinner was of the reconstituted variety, brought back to life in a Styrofoam cup with boiling water, but it was hot and better than expected. There had been some improvement over the noodles and bouillon cube dinners he'd had in the past. Not much, but some.

He doctored the mashed potatoes with salt, pepper and garlic packets he had kept from previous take-out stops, and paired the potatoes with some beef jerky and nuts. He did his best to finish the trip as empty-handed as he had started.

He slept fitfully that night. This journey would be over soon, and he would be going home. Of course, his mind was filled with all that that meant.

XXVII

He woke early, without an alarm clock in sight. That was something he was really going to miss.

Mike took his time breaking camp. The finality of it all made him pause and hesitate over each step, but it was also such a short ride to the finish that there was no need to rush. He packed things with a little more care this morning, as if they would be stored away for some time.

He realized that he had only experienced one day of significant rain on the way down and offered up thanks to whoever might be listening. He had dutifully packed away everything in plastic bags for protection, and maybe that was enough to cosmically ensure that there would be little rain.

Once he was all packed up and ready to hit the road, he indulged himself with a walk before hopping on the bike. There was no special feature of this campsite like a lake or viewpoint to draw him, so he walked aimlessly through the woods. The sun had not yet burned off the mist that clung to the tree tops, but it was already warm enough to walk without a jacket.

He walked along the camp roads scanning the underbrush and treetops for something unique to that place. It felt like he had to say "thank you" and "goodbye" to the trees, and he wanted to pay attention and homage to what he was leaving behind. He picked up a smooth stone that lay in the middle of the road and rubbed his thumb absently across its surface as he walked in meditation.

After about a half hour of walking, he found himself back at his own campsite. It was time to break the reminiscent spell and get moving on down the road.

He threw his leg over the top tube of his bike and took one last look around. When he put his hands on the handlebars, he realized he was still carrying the small stone. His arm was halfway through the throwing motion, before he stopped and slipped the stone into his jersey pocket. He said one more "thank you," out loud this time, before pedaling out to the main road.

The road through the woods would actually take him back to Highway 101. Just a few miles later, 101 would join up with Highway 1 and both roads would take him over the Golden Gate Bridge. It was a nice bit of symbolism that the two main roads that carried him down the coast would come together to usher him to the finish.

The road out of camp climbed slowly for the first few miles. The slope was not difficult, but it reminded him to take it slow this morning. The road was quiet, and the shoulder was wide and smooth. He had come to appreciate the quality of the road surface like never before, and he imagined that he would now notice shoulder width and steepness of slope even when driving in a car.

He thought about Gerry again. He had obviously inspired this trip, and it felt like he had been riding alongside as a guide. He had such an impact for someone Michael he had only seen a handful of times, and it was still hard to believe he was gone.

He remembered that Gerry and his group of riders had stopped in Sausalito for "second breakfast" before heading into San Francisco. It was one last time for all of them to gather together, and one last chance to delay the end. Mike planned to stop for breakfast there as well, to honor Gerry and to prolong the end of his own journey.

He found a great breakfast place right on the main road. There was outdoor seating overlooking a marina, and the skyline was peppered with sailboat masts hypnotically lolling on the gentle water. At first, the interior of the restaurant seemed much less peaceful. The place was huge, but nearly every available chair was filled, and a long line of people snaked from the counter to the door, queued up for caffeine and sustenance.

Although the line was long, everyone seemed to be happy to wait. No one was talking on a Bluetooth headset or tapping away on a Blackberry, content to avoid multitasking for now. The people behind the counter had a great, positive energy, and it seemed to carry over to all the patrons.

The menu boasted several interesting items, most with certified organic ingredients, but Mike ordered a pretty basic breakfast bagel sandwich with his coffee. Once it was all ready, he found an open table outside and settled in to enjoy the sunshine.

He shared the patio with several people in business attire, but again they seemed to be willing to take the extra ten minutes to enjoy their breakfast rather than wolfing it down on the run. His return to society was being phased in quite nicely. He offered up a toast to Gerry and his memory, raising his cup of coffee to the sky.

After finishing his breakfast and second cup of coffee, he felt like he could not stretch out the morning any longer without somehow tarnishing it. After a visit to the restroom, he mounted his bike one last time and took to the road. He was only a few miles from the end, so he pedaled slowly.

Within minutes, his eyes were watering. Several wonderful things were coming to an end, and the difficulty of what lay ahead carried its own weight. Soon he saw the red metal girders of the bridge towering on the horizon and knew he was moments away from the finish.

He had not really thought about how special it would be to cross the Golden Gate Bridge at the end of his journey. It was a symbol of the city and even the nation, and brought forth a certain amount of pride even for an out-of-towner. Of course its crossing from a sleepy town to the big city was also an apt metaphor of crossing back into the real world after his two weeks away from the business of society.

There was a parking area just short of the bridge, and he pulled over to hesitate for one last moment. It was also a great place to get some initial photos of the bridge. After snapping a number of shots of the bridge, he asked a nearby tourist to take a picture of him and his bike with the bridge as a backdrop.

He disconnected his bike from the trailer and hoisted it up over his head as if he were a conquering hero. He had a photo of Gerry in a similar pose, and it would end up being one of his favorite photos.

After he could delay no longer, he pedaled his bike onto the sidewalk of the bridge. The sidewalk was wide and bordered on both sides with protective fences. Every ten feet or so, he passed twin cables rising vertically from the roadway to the arcing cables suspended by the two towers. It really was an elegant way to span such great distances.

The fog that San Francisco is notorious for was not in evidence, having either burned off or not rolled in just yet. He was on the east side of the road, so he had a wonderful view of Alcatraz and the city, but he could also see across the bridge to the bay inlet on his right. He had not realized how high up the bridge was, and it gave him one of those small twinges of wanting to turn into the abyss.

There had been a sign at the entrance to the bridge that told you which side of the bridge to bike on, depending on what time of day it was. Bikes rode on the east side in the morning and the west in the evenings.

It didn't make much sense to him to move them back and forth, or to have them biking in opposite directions on the same sidewalk, but he assumed it had to do something with bridge upkeep. He remembered seeing a TV show following maintenance crews as they shimmied up the arcing cables to paint or replace lights. He couldn't imagine working that high up, and was happy to give them all the room they needed.

The bridge was a bit longer than a mile and a half in length, and he pedaled so slowly that it took him ten minutes to cross. There were a number of other pedestrians and bikers out, most going in the opposite direction. It was a bit crowded having two-way traffic on the sidewalk, but most everyone was going slowly enough that there were no issues. Many of the bikers were riding hybrid bikes with a rental company's logo prominently displayed on the front bag.

He finally reached the south side of the bridge and was officially in San Francisco. He coasted down the path, looping around to the bay side of the park. He found another parking lot on this side of the bridge and pulled over. From this vantage point he could see the whole bridge in profile. The bridge now held a certain significance to him, and he would end up with many shots from multiple angles.

He eventually put his camera away and just stared at the bridge. It was hard to believe that he had pedaled his way down the coast from Seattle in two weeks. He looked down at his bike computer and cycled through the screens until he found the odometer. It showed that he had biked 960 miles over 13 days. A silly part of him wanted to bike another 40 so he could crack the 1000 mile mark.

This part of his journey was at an end. So much loomed ahead of him, but he did not want to think about that right now. He just wanted to stay in the moment and acknowledge what he had been through, and what he had accomplished already.

He sat down on the grassy hillside and cried for a while. About everything.

XXVIII

He eventually gathered himself up and pedaled on down the road. He found a visitor's center nearby and was pointed in the direction of a relatively inexpensive hotel. It was still pricier than he wanted, but apparently you don't stay cheaply in San Francisco. After checking into the hotel and maneuvering his bike and trailer combo up to his room, he took a nice long shower.

He filled the bathtub up afterward and used it as a laundry tub. He decided he did not want to spend the afternoon cooling his heels in a Laundromat for half a load of clothes. He had to keep moving.

After washing his stuff out and hanging it up to dry on the shower rod, he took out his laptop and got online.

The first order of business was a way home. He found a ticket on a discount airline for an afternoon flight the following day. It would give him little more than 24 hours in the city, but that felt about right.

He called a few bike shops and asked them how much it would be to ship his bike back home. It would be easier than checking it as luggage, and the few extra dollars to ship it was worth the avoided hassle. He got directions to the shop with the best price and made an appointment for the following morning.

He looked up a couple of other addresses and with some streetcar routes plotted out, he went back out to the city. It seemed a shame not to see at least part of the city before he headed home. He had grabbed a couple of brochures while he was at the visitor's center, and he decided to start at Pier 39.

According to the pamphlet, Pier 39 had a variety of restaurants and shops, but the chief attraction was the sea lions. For reasons that weren't entirely clear, a large group (herd, pack, pod, gaggle?) of sea lions called the pier area home.

In 1989, when the boats moored at the marina were temporarily moved out to refurbish the dock, the sea lions moved in. When the dock upgrades were finished, the sea lions had staked their claim and eventually chased most of the boats out. In the end, the sea lions probably drew enough tourists to offset the lost mooring fees.

The sea lions of Pier 39 were an impressive sight. A few were swimming in the little bay protected by a concrete breakwater, but a hundred or more were fighting for dock space to lounge in the sun. Well *fighting* wasn't exactly correct, as most seemed content to lie skin to skin on the small floating docks, their seemingly boneless bodies spread across the weathered wood planks.

There was a line of tourists leaning against the pier railing, snapping photos of the piles of blubbery bodies, probably a little envious of how the sea lions lounged in the sun without a care.

The shopping area of the pier was a dramatic contrast of busy activity. Mike wandered by the store fronts, looking for nothing in particular and only venturing inside a few of the shops. He was mostly people watching as he walked up and down the promenade.

After two weeks on the road, riding alone through much smaller towns, the crowds of San Francisco soon became overwhelming. He ducked into a restaurant to have a bite of lunch, and the relative calm of the place was soothing. Those sea lions had the right idea – take it slow, lounge when you can.

After lunch he walked toward Fisherman's Wharf. When he looked up things to do in San Francisco, Fisherman's Wharf was one of the first things to pop up, but it was really just another shopping and restaurant district as far as Mike could tell.

Uninterested in further window shopping, he continued walking and found a public beach just to the west.

The beach was called the Aquatic Park and the little cove was protected by a curving breakwater. There was a dock to the right of the beach with a three-masted wooden ship tied up on the near side. It was a cool looking boat, and Mike wondered if it was still in use. He had seen old ships turned into floating restaurants in other places, but this one looked to still be seaworthy, and might be one of the many ways to tour the bay.

He kicked off his shoes and walked barefoot on the sand. There were a number of small buoys that looked like some sort of course for swimmers or kayakers, but no one was out on the water today. Sea gulls wandering the water's edge, outnumbering people in this little oasis. The San Francisco waterfront seemed to be a nice balance of human busyness and animal calm.

Mike walked into the water and the cold enveloped his sore legs. He could see the Golden Gate Bridge over the breakwater, and the sight of it took him away again. He felt a calm wash over him like the waves tickling at his legs, and he decided that this was as much of the city as he needed to see. He might return one day to see all the sights, but this was enough this time around.

While he stood in the water, he thought about the ocean itself. It was a near constant companion on his trip, and staring at the endless horizon while the biting cold surf crashed around his feet had become his healing ritual.

He hadn't really thought about it before talking to Erin the other night, but he had basically ended up at the ocean that first night in West Seattle. Without really thinking of where to go after finding the note, he was drawn to the sands and salt water of Alki Beach. He supposed the sounds of the waves were there in the background when he pulled himself back from the ledge.

He walked around in the water and along the sand for about a half an hour before deciding to head back. He used an outdoor shower to wash the sand from his feet and then walked back out to the relative chaos of the street.

Back at the hotel, he maneuvered his bike and trailer back down to the street and headed off. He pedaled to one of the addresses he had looked up earlier, and it turned out to be only a few blocks west of the Aquatic Park he had been at just an hour before.

He pulled up to the building and locked his bike to a nearby metal post before heading inside. After wandering around for a bit, and asking some questions of the person behind the counter, he came back outside. He unhitched the trailer from the bike and wheeled it inside the Goodwill Donation Center.

The trailer would not be making the trip home with him, and he trusted that Goodwill would find it a new home for a new child. He exchanged the trailer for a duffel bag and some extra cash, trading his vision of family and home for the transience of single life.

XXIX

The next morning he rode to the bicycle shop to get his bike packed for shipping.

The guys at the shop were helpful and friendly, and he felt much more at home here than any of the shops he had walked into yesterday. Being bikers themselves, they were of course interested in Michael's story and he ended up chatting with them for nearly an hour about his trip. He eventually had to head back to the hotel, and they wished him well, promising to take good care of his bike.

He had packed the night before, so there wasn't much left to do but head for the airport. One of the BART trains went directly to the airport, and it was a relatively short walk from the hotel to a station. He hauled his backpack and large duffel bag onto the train and found a seat by a window.

As he watched the city of San Francisco whiz by, he wished Seattle had a similar sort of train system. There had been talk about light rail for decades, and it was only now getting any traction. Traffic may have finally reached a point where people were sufficiently fed up to take the plunge.

He was a couple hours early for his flight, so after checking his duffel bag he found a seat at one of the airport bars. After he got home he would have to stop eating out so much for both financial and health reasons, but he was still in vacation mode. He ordered a Jack & Coke and a burger. He felt like he had been reasonably controlled about his drinking on this trip, all things considered, but he would have to keep an eye on that as well.

He pulled out his notebook, wondering how much time or motivation he would have to write when he was back in the routine of his life. Of course, he realized that there was nothing routine waiting for him at home. A good portion of his life would never be the same. He wished this was all some TV dream sequence that he would snap out of. That his dog would wake him from a nap on the couch, and Katelyn would tell him with a smile that he had been talking in his sleep. But his life was not the stuff of movies.

His plane ride was uneventful, and his checked bag had made the flight home as well. Not ready to face anyone just yet, he took an airport shuttle home rather than call a friend for a ride. The specter of his empty household loomed ahead of him, and he didn't want anyone looking over his shoulder or trying to comfort him when he faced it for the second time. His first reflex was still to keep things to himself. He knew it had to change, but not for this.

The airport shuttle took a meandering route to his house, dropping off other passengers along the way. He was the northernmost passenger of the group, so he was the last one left in the van when it pulled up to the curb by the house.

He tipped the driver and stood on the front lawn staring at the front door. The van pulled away and the only sounds he could hear were the cars on the highway a half a mile away. The distant sound of rubber meeting and leaving the road sounded a bit like the ocean and that somehow helped him gather the strength to walk in.

~

The next three months were the most difficult.

The house looked the same as it did before heading out on his two week runaway bike ride. He had imagined several things as he turned the handle of the front door. Did Katelyn come back to trash the place or clean it out? Was she even aware that he was gone? He had made no effort to contact her while he was riding down the coast, and he wondered what his silence had made her think.

The house was just as he had left it. The air was a bit stale after two weeks, and it made the empty feeling that much more palpable. When he opened the door to her room and found it half empty, it crushed out the last flicker of belief that it had all been a dream.

After only ten minutes, he was ready to leave again. It felt like it was some sort of exposure therapy to rid himself of an allergy, and he would take slowly increasing doses of pain until his body no longer reacted.

But he had a good excuse to leave the first time. He wanted to get his dog.

His dog would be one of his greatest allies over the next year. After bringing her home, the house was no longer empty. She was there to give him love, but more importantly to receive Michael's love. By taking care of her, he was taking care of himself.

He would break down in tears many times over the next few months, and her presence soothed him like no words could ever do. In fact, in those moments, words were the last thing he wanted to hear. He didn't want sympathy, commiseration, or words of encouragement when he was at his lowest; he just wanted the quiet presence of love.

Even the most enlightened person will make some small judgment when someone else is falling to pieces. It was much easier for Michael to break down in front of his dog.

But he could no longer shut himself off from the world. That was a big part of why he was in this situation, and he did not want to live that way any longer. In truth, Katelyn's leaving stripped him bare of any pride he thought he was due, and made it a bit easier to share that part of his life that he had previously locked away. And having to tell his story to so many friends and family, he became more open through sheer repetition.

He began with the couple that had been watching their dog. If he had been forced to come up with some sort of perverted ranking of who deserved to be told first, they would not have been on top. But they were the first people he encountered, and there was no reason to put it off by lying to them. It was certainly not an honor for them, he was sure.

He didn't bother to ask what Katelyn had told them two weeks earlier when she dropped off the dog. Although this wasn't their problem, they had a certain stake in the marriage like any friend does. He didn't want to put them in the middle of things, forcing them to decide what to reveal or whether to lie. He stumbled his way through a brief summation of what had gone on the last two weeks with the promise that he would tell them more when he could.

The story was never easy to tell, but it was more difficult with certain people. He dreaded telling his parents the most, and his brother offered to be there with him when he broke the news. They were amazingly understanding and offered as much support as he needed. They did not immediately flip to speaking badly of Katelyn, and he found comfort in that somehow. Once he told his parents, it was a fraction easier to tell other people.

He had chosen not to share the contents of the note, the infidelity or the chance that she was pregnant. For some reason that was somehow irrelevant when he was telling people that their marriage was over. As disgusting as the ending had been to him, he had loved her for many years and wasn't ready to destroy the memories just yet.

When he picked up the stack of mail at the post office, there was a letter from Katelyn's lawyer. It was mostly boilerplate and introductory B.S., essentially telling him that proceedings were being set in motion.

He eventually received an e-mail from Katelyn. It was not venomous like her note had been, and actually lacked much emotion at all. She made it very clear that she had no interest in discussing their marriage and was primarily concerned with making dissolution as smooth as possible.

She proposed a general outline of what she wanted and was willing to give up. She wasn't asking for much. He didn't know if she was being generous or just wanted nothing to interfere with the clean slate she was trying to create. She arranged for a time where she could come and pick up her parents' things that were stacked in the garage, and she asked that Mike not be around.

He would be left guessing about pretty much everything. About all he had to go on were the note and his own impressions of what went wrong. It was no surprise that there was no communication between them now, as this seemed to be one of the biggest problems with their marriage. He had been shocked out of his stupor and was ready to talk, but she was not interested. Everything unsaid, remained unsaid.

They would sell the house. She did not want it, and he could not afford it on his own. She had taken very little of their mutual belongings, and he would sell or give away much of them. He had no idea where he was going to live once the house sold, but he knew he would be downsizing dramatically.

Although they had bought much of the furniture together, it was really just stuff to him and it wasn't that difficult to list it for sale. It was when he started packing away the pictures and other totems of their life together that he was brought to tears and left curled up on the floor.

~

A month or so after his return, he decided to go to a counselor.

He had told his story countless times to friends and family, but he felt that he needed more help. He needed both a professional, as well as someone neutral. As open as he tried to be, there were certain things that he was unable or unwilling to discuss with friends. He needed someone out of his inner circle that he could talk to about the things he was too ashamed to discuss elsewhere.

He had never had any interest in seeking professional help before. His "bootstraps" personality did not allow for it. He felt like he should be able to figure things out for himself, and that paying someone to nod and say "hmm" was a waste of time. Not surprisingly, Mike had no clue what he was talking about.

The simple act of trying to explain the whole story to a stranger helped him to focus his thinking. With the counselor, he had to start at the beginning, talking about his own history and not just the marriage and aftermath. They dug deeper to the core of who he was, and why he behaved the way he did.

When he could not explain or justify his crippling feelings of shame, they seemed less legitimate. He carried tremendous guilt for failures that seemed trivial when he was forced to say them out loud. He had been beating himself up for so long it had become a habit, and the shame found a life of its own, independent of reason.

The counselor gave him the insight of an outside observer, and without trivializing his feelings, helped Mike understand how out of proportion his reactions were.

The more time he spent talking with the counselor, the more he realized how messed up he had become. He had internalized things thinking he was being strong, but came to realize how foolish that impression was. Ironically, it takes a certain amount of strength to show your weaknesses to others. And in trying to hide away his weaknesses, he had become less human.

Katelyn clearly had her own faults and a hand in the failure of the marriage, but for the first few months Mike focused only on what he had done wrong. He was encouraged to drop the words *wrong*, *fault* and *blame* from his vocabulary, but he resisted. He wanted reasons; he wanted to know what mistakes were made.

But even if he knew, he was helpless to change anything they had done in the past, and that was the most difficult thing to let go. All he could do was change what he did moving forward and how he maintained his remaining relationships.

He felt completely exposed during counseling and now was the time to dig into things before he could revert to his self-protective ways. He continued to work through his feelings of guilt and shame to try to pull himself back to the world. Anger would come much later, and he would find some strength there as well.

~

He tried to keep moving.

He had found a certain amount of momentum from the trip, and he did not want to let it dissipate. Admittedly, sometimes the constant motion was to distract him from the pain, but it also helped to bring some order to a life turned upside down.

He was latching onto quotes these days, trying to use these brief bits of wisdom to find some clarity, and there was an appropriate one by Albert Einstein, "Life is like riding a bicycle – in order to keep your balance, you must keep moving."

When he became overwhelmed with thoughts and emotions, he fell back on another technique from the ride. When the voices of failures from the past became too loud, he would repeat the mantra of "Focus, Focus, Focus" until he brought himself back to the present. The mantra helped him here just as it did while struggling up a difficult hill.

Once the painful task of packing away the personal items was completed, he threw himself into preparing the house for sale. He held a couple of garage sales and sold other things online. Once the house was less cluttered, he set about making the house as attractive as possible.

They didn't want to spend much money on fixing up the house, so it was mostly cleaning and painting. When he looked at the house through the eyes of a potential buyer, he realized how much stuff they had let slide. He could not work on the years of deferred maintenance in their relationship, but he found some satisfaction in taking care of the neglect evident in the house.

He continued to see his counselor.

There were times when he felt guilty speaking about the pain he was going through. He rationalized that over half of marriages fail. Theirs was no more special than any other, and neither was his pain. He was just a statistic.

But he could not reason his way out of this hole with math or logic. He was encouraged to accept that his pain was his own, and it was valid, regardless of how many other people suffered in the same way.

His emotions cycled like never before. It left him feeling unstable, but more alive and open to clarity. At times it felt like a door opened in his mind, and a rush of light shot out, meeting the light of the world pushing its way in. Stoicism would rise up and depressive thoughts threw their weight against the door to slam it shut. He couldn't always hold them back, but he could at least stick a rock in the jam to keep a small crack open for shafts of light to pass through.

Each session brought out more pain and tears, but he left feeling a little better each time. Misery expressed is misery reduced, or something like that. He had to admit that talking to someone brought more relief than just writing about it. But he continued to write just the same.

~

Six months after his return, the house was sold, but the divorce was not yet final. They had to wait for a blood test.

It turned out that Katelyn was pregnant after all. She was certain it was not Mike's, but a DNA test would make the dissolution paperwork much clearer. As much as he had wanted a child, he secretly hoped that she was correct that it was not his. He wondered how could she be so sure? In one of the rare moments of disclosure, she told him.

They had stopped "trying" a couple of months before she left him, but that was cutting it a little fine to be so sure who the father was. She confessed that after the first month of their trying to get pregnant, she moved their baby-making efforts to the wrong time in her cycle. She was not planning on getting pregnant with the man she was having an affair with, but she was nearly certain that the baby was a result of an affair accident rather than a husband's efforts.

The one kernel of truth Katelyn offered left him obsessing once more over the question of *why*. He recognized their shortcomings and shouldered much of the blame for the state of their marriage, but what was it that made her decide that the marriage was beyond repair? Was it something he or they could have fixed, or was it something in their personalities she thought was impossible to change? Was it something trivial or monumental that was the final straw? How could he not have seen it?

He would reach for a memory to explain it all, only to watch it retreat from his grasp. The more he searched, the more it became clear that it was not just the recent fugue states that created blank spaces in his history. Much of the details of the last decade were hazy or missing. The depressive fog he had walked around in had prevented any details from imprinting. He imagined it to be similar to the side effects of being on bipolar medication. Every edge is dulled, every feeling muted.

The mind naturally filters through information, tuning out what it deems unimportant. If your brain registered every sound, every texture, every blip of information – if it picked up every mechanical click, every voice, every intake of breath – it would drive you insane. The brain attempts to see the overall picture without singling out every pixel. But Michael's brain seemed to have gone much further, shutting out most of life. He felt like he had just woken from a coma, with only vague impressions left from someone whispering at his bedside.

He had several theories that he tried to hang the divorce on, but none of them seemed to quite fit. The best he could come up with was that once they started trying to have children, she felt that it was her last chance to get out relatively unscathed. But it didn't really explain the why, only the when.

~

A year after he found the note, he had a new life. The divorce was final, and the blood test confirmed that the child was not his.

He had given up on the sales job he was ill-suited for. He wasn't a salesman, and working from home was no longer important to him now that children were out of the picture. What he needed was security, a steady income and the safety net of health insurance.

He worked in a coffee shop that provided insurance for even part-time workers. Coffee houses had always been his home away from home, and he found that he really enjoyed being on the other side of the counter. The interaction with the endless line of people coming in for their daily caffeine fix kept him from retreating too far back into his shell.

He also made a concerted effort to see his friends often. It was difficult at times as he was the only unmarried person in the group, but they did everything they could to make him feel included and welcome. The more time he spent with those he loved, the clearer it became how much he had distanced himself with feelings of shame and failure. He did not want to ever go back there again.

He moved into a ground floor apartment about half an hour north of the city. The place was kind of small but he kept it lightly furnished so it did not feel cramped. He wanted to carry around less stuff, and that started at home.

He had a storage unit where he kept the memories of his marriage. He did not want them close at hand, but he did not want to discard them either. His wedding ring was one of the few things he kept at the apartment, tucked away in a tiny box out of sight.

Once he had settled in, he printed out pictures and put them in frames. He wanted them off his computer and onto the walls, out of the deeper reaches of his brain and out into world. He needed to see the faces and places of his fonder memories, so that each morning he would be reminded of all he had to be thankful for.

There were also several pictures of road signs on his wall. There were elevation signs from the peaks he had climbed, others with varying distances to San Francisco, and of course the "Lane Ends, Merge Left" sign from Gerry's jersey.

In one picture, the top sign was a black drawing of a bicycle on a yellow background, with a sign below that told drivers to "Share the Road". It was a visual reminder of his new mantra, and the way he wanted to live his life moving forward.

The ground floor apartment made it easier on the dog, and he actually had a little fenced off area about the size of a small bedroom out back. He also tried to take the pooch out for a daily walk for both of their sakes.

And he kept biking. He found the time on the road to be therapeutic. Whenever he felt stressed or depressed, riding his bike seemed to help. The physical activity seemed to relieve the tension, and the time alone on the road helped him sort out the thoughts that sometimes overwhelmed him. He rode it to work most days, and he felt more connected to the world during his commute than when he was wrapped in steel and glass.

He still broke down occasionally when he thought about his marriage, but the episodes became less frequent and less intense. The details of memory seem to lose distinction over time, and eventually come together like beads of mercury to form a sphere of pure feeling. Pain came less as a stab to the brain, more often felt as a weight on his heart.

He still stumbled over words like "their" and "our" when he spoke, and saying "ex-wife" left a bitter taste in his mouth. He didn't think he would ever forget the failure of their marriage, or forgive either one of them for their hand in it, but the significance in his daily life grew smaller with time.

But even that made him feel a little guilty for a while. It was like he needed to mourn the loss sufficiently, and the duration and level of pain had to match his previous feelings of love. It was like some sort of self-imposed penance. He had not entirely broken the habit of over-thinking, but he was at least better at realizing how ridiculous it was at times.

When he wasn't working, biking or spending time with friends, he continued to write. It brought him solace in its own way, and a measure of pride that he maintained the habit he had dropped ten years before. Where he used to hide in his writing, putting things in writing instead of saying them out loud, it now felt like it connected him with the world.

He had started writing online, and tried to put up a post every day. In order to have something to write about, it forced him to pay more attention to the world around him and keep the mental fog at bay. He reserved his thoughts about his marriage for the notebook he started on his bike trip. He had inklings that he might put it into book form someday, but for now it was for himself alone.

He was writing in the notebook after work one afternoon and saw that he was about out of paper. Though he had continued to write after he returned from the trip, he had been writing in the notebook less often. But it felt like he had more to say, so he would need to pick up a new one soon.

When he reached the last page, he noticed that there was some writing on the back of it. He turned the page and found a note from Erin. It had to have been written a year ago, but he had never noticed it before. It read:

> You seem like a special man who has lost his way. I am sorry that you are going through all this, but I hope that you find your way back someday. I would love to hear from you when you do.
> Erin.

Below her name was her phone number. He had never forgotten about her or the night they had spent together. It felt like she had appeared in his life at the time of his greatest need. Serendipity or guardian angel, he had never wanted to examine it too closely. She had been the first to hear the whole story, and by telling her it was his first small step back toward the life he had left behind.

He had sent her an e-mail when he reached San Francisco, but in the tumult of returning home, he had not written or heard from her since. He assumed that she had vanished from his life in the same way she had suddenly appeared.

But here she was, reaching out again and making him believe in some sort of invisible hand behind the mystery.

He closed the notebook with a smile. He grabbed the leash and took his dog for a walk, slipping his phone and that last page into his pocket on the way out the door.

ACKNOWLEDGMENTS

This book is a work of fiction. Like any author, my life and experiences have informed the story. People who know me may recognize scenic details along the way, and I hope that only adds to the story. But the story is a work of fiction, and the characters and their actions are not based on anyone I know.

Gerry, however, is based on a real person. The details in the story are fictitious, but I hope I have honored him with the portrayal here.

I have ended up where I am by a series of gentle (and not so gentle) shoves from both friends and the universe. As I have said elsewhere, I am not the river carving its way through the landscape. I am more like driftwood that finds its path by following the current and bouncing off the obstacles along the way. Friends and family have been there to push me out of the shallows and hand me an oar now and then. I would not be who I am without you. You are too numerous to mention here, so know that I am talking to you when I say – thank you and I love you.

I would, however, like to thank Sean Hawkins specifically for giving me the shove I needed to finally put something in book form.

I would also like to thank NaNoWriMo.org for their sponsoring of National Novel Writing Month each November. They get hundreds of thousands of would-be-authors off the sidelines to tell their story. To stop looking for that perfect pen or piece of software that will make it all suddenly happen. To change "someday" to "I did it!"

The challenge of writing 50,000 words in the span of 30 days encourages you to shut off that little voice that says you will never write anything worth reading. Of course, what you have at the end of thirty days is NOT worth reading. The editing and rewriting period was different kind of adventure, and it was the grinding marathon to the thirty day sprint of the first draft.

I would like to thank my beta readers for helping me to see what worked and what didn't. For pointing out typos, punctuation errors, and for doing what Word can't, like catching "decent" when it was supposed to be "descent". Most of all, I want to thank them for the encouragement to carry on when I was unsure the story was worth telling. So thank you to Sean H, Kristy, Matt, Holly, Diane, Alice, and of course Mom & Dad. Thank you for seeing things that I couldn't, and for helping me to improve - for that is what it is all about.

As a self-published author, I depend on the word of mouth and social media to spread the word. I would appreciate any time you take to recommend or review my novel on Amazon, Facebook, Good Reads or elsewhere. So, thank you dear reader for taking this journey with me. I hope you enjoyed it as much as I did.

And a final thank you to coffee shops everywhere, and especially the Starbucks in Lemon Grove, CA. Thanks for all the strong coffee, chocolate chip cookies, and for being my home-away-from-home office.

ABOUT THE AUTHOR

Sean grew up in Washington, but is currently living in California with the best dog on earth. He has ridden his bike in some amazing places, and encourages everyone to take the opportunity to see the world from this perspective. As Hemmingway said, "It is by riding a bicycle that you learn the contours of a country best."

Share the Road was Sean's debut novel, and it was self-published New Year's Day 2012. He continues to try and write his way out of corners, and you can find him online at ViewsFromTwoWheels.com, and at SeanDay.net.

Made in the USA
Las Vegas, NV
20 February 2023

67854861R00121